MW00426240

A WILDE PLAYERS DIRTY ROMANCE

USA Today Bestselling Authors
A.M. HARGROVE
& TERRI E. LAINE

Published By Wicked Truth Publishing, LLC
Copyright © 2016 A.M. Hargrove and Terri E. Laine
All rights reserved.
This book is protected under the copyright laws of the United
States of America.
No part of this publication may be reproduced, distributed, or
transmitted in any form or by any means, including photocopying,
recording, or other electronic or mechanical methods, without the
prior written permission of the author, except in the case of brief
quotations embodied in critical reviews and certain other
noncommercial uses permitted by copyright law. For permission
requests, write to the author, addressed "Attention: Permissions
Coordinator," at HargroveLaineBooks@gmail.com

This is a work of fiction. Any resemblance to peoples either living
or deceased is purely coincidental. Names, places, and characters
are figments of the author's imagination, or, if real, used
fictitiously.

Cover by Michele Catalano - Creative

Cover photo by Wander Aguiar

ISBN-13: 9781536907216

ISBN: 1536907219

DEDICATION

This one is dedicated to women who love to watch hot men play sports and to the hot men who love to play them.

FLETCHER

Gray skies and snow flurries greet me as I reach for the handle to exit my old truck. "Boomer, Brady, you fellas stay. You hear me?" Two sets of sad eyes and two wet black noses crowd me by the door. It's a miracle we all fit in the front seat. I can't figure out how my dad does it. When I was getting ready to drive into town, no sooner had I opened the truck door and they jumped inside. No amount of coaxing would get them out.

After I park and open the door, Boomer tries to nudge his way out. "Boomer, stay. I'm running across the street to buy you some food, you doofus. You eat like a horse." Brady, Boomer's best friend, doesn't like that, so he lets out a yap, and then both of them are making such a ruckus, everyone on the street stares at us.

"Would you guys keep it down? I'll be right back." Pushing Boomer's large furry face back inside, I close the door and lean on the truck for a second. You'd have thought my dad would have stocked the house with at least more than one day's worth of food for his ravenous pups. But no. Here I am, six thirty at night, running out to buy them more chow.

I navigate the slippery streets while taking a glance or two back at the yipping dogs in my truck. *This should be a quick trip*, I think to myself.

Twenty-five seconds. That's all it should've taken me to cross the street and get inside. Maybe not even that. In the time it takes to huddle, get set up, and snap a ball, squealing tires and the roar of an engine change everything. Glancing in the direction of the sound, I see headlights barreling down on me a second too late. I feel like I'm stuck in the mud, my feet cemented to concrete slabs, as I'm blinded by the beams.

Pain explodes in my leg before gravity is no longer a factor, and I'm flying like fucking Superman. Instead of being straight, I'm flipping end over end, before I slam back down to earth—or rather a car—as my shoulder, or as my agent would say, *my million-dollar-throwing arm*, connects with the windshield. Something cracks. And then for seconds, minutes, hours—there's nothing. I have no idea until I blink because the sound of people yelling from somewhere off in the distance pulls me back. Apparently, after that last hit, I tumbled off the car and slammed into the street.

No one has to tell me this is bad or that my right arm is completely fucked. In twenty-five seconds, my entire life is altered, ripped away, and reconstructed into something I'd never expected, didn't plan for, and certainly didn't want. And worse, the shouts increase as the motherfucker that hit me reverses with spinning tires before he peels off like Dale Earnhardt, Jr. And how I remain conscious and can recall this with brutal clarity, I have no damn idea.

Lightning strikes every nerve ending in my body, igniting it with fire. I know pain more than I care to admit. As the starting quarterback for the Oklahoma Rockets, I deal with it nearly every day. But this is an entirely new level. I can't begin to pinpoint its origination because it's coming from every-fucking-where. I feel like the guy at the bottom of the pile holding the ball everyone's scrambling to get.

In the distance, there are shouts to call 911. Not much later, I can hear sirens in the distance. But not for long. Everything dims, and the next thing I recall is waking up in the hospital with my Aunt Shelly staring at me.

"What's …?" I try to say, but my throat scratches like sandpaper.

"Fletcher, honey, you're awake. Do you know what happened?" When I only groan, she adds, "You got hit by a car and are in the hospital. But you're going to be fine. The doctor will be here shortly."

Fine. That's easy for her to say because I don't feel *fine* at all.

"Did you drive here all the way from Raleigh?"

Which was a dumb question because, of course, she did.

"Yes, and I should call your parents."

"Don't," I grumble.

"They should know," she protests.

"I'm not a child. I'm here to watch their house while they're on a much needed long vacation. Besides, they need to spend time with my brother, which they rarely have the opportunity to do. No need to worry them."

She sighs and opens her mouth to gripe at me some more. But as if she's conjured him, the doctor strides in, and then I wish he hadn't. He's not exactly smiling when he enters.

"Mr. Wilde, I'm Dr. Logan, and I have good news and bad. The best is that you are alive." I huff because I don't exactly believe him, not if he says what I'm expecting to hear. "And you're lucky that your head, neck, and spine were spared. You'll have no lasting effects from the accident. You're going to feel pretty sore for a while, though, because you took a definite beating. However ..."

And I know the shit ain't good, like the view of a three hundred fifty pound lineman barreling down on me just as I'm about to throw the ball. The way the doctor's eyes pull down tells me more than what I'm prepared to hear.

"You sustained a very severe shoulder separation that will require surgery, along with an ACL tear that we'll have to repair. We need to wait for the swelling to subside before we do anything, though. We can do that here, or you can elect to have it done by a surgeon of your choice. But I wouldn't suggest waiting. It can be done here in a week or so. We'll send you home tomorrow, and you can come back for the other procedure. It'll be outpatient. And because I know who you are... I'm afraid it's probable that you will be out for most, if not all, of the coming season."

Fuck me. Football is my life, my reason for being. I can't imagine sitting on the sidelines just as my career is really taking off. And what the hell am I going to tell my agent, coach, manager, the president, and owner of my team? *Hey, guess what? Your QB got hit by a car while buying dog food.* Then I start laughing. Of all the things in my contract that I can't do, such as snow skiing, riding a scooter, a dirt bike, or mountain biking, one of the things they forgot to add was crossing the street to buy fucking dog food.

"Fletcher, are you okay?"

I want to say *what in the fucking hell do you think?* Instead, I shake my head and say, "I'll survive."

Aunt Shelly pats my good arm and says, "Don't worry, kiddo. It's only one season, and you'll be back better than ever."

"Yeah," I say, swallowing my bitterness. What they don't know is this is my contract year. If I sit out, I'll get royally screwed right up the ol' ass. And all because of a bag of fucking dog food.

"Mr. Wilde, now that you're awake, the police are here to ask you a few questions. They've been waiting."

"Police?"

"Yes," the doctor answers. "Since you were hit by a car, and the driver left the scene, it's considered a felony."

"I see."

The doctor stands there and stares. Then it registers that he's waiting for me to give my permission. "Yeah, fine. They can come in."

He opens the door, and a couple of guys in uniform shuffle in. They tell me how sorry they are about the accident and then ask me what I remember. Closing my eyes, I give them my twenty-five second replay of the ugly scene. All of the important facts, such as the make of the car, the color, and the license plate number are nonexistent in my mind. Basically, I'm no help whatsoever. After shaking my left hand, they leave.

As time passes, it doesn't take long for everyone to see that I'm a dick—a fucking assface and a terrible overall patient. After Aunt Shelly gets me back home, it only takes a day for her not to want to put up with my sorry ass anymore and ends up firing herself as my nurse. She hightails it back to Raleigh and her family once she hires someone to take over for her.

Now I have Rita, a tiny woman who could fit inside a shoebox, taking care of me. And I'm six and a half feet tall. Not to mention that woman is a saint. I don't know how she puts up with my jackhole moods, but she does. I'm cranky and foul-tempered as I struggle with needing someone else's help.

"No, Mr. Fletcher, you mustn't—" she wags a finger at me when I try to get out of bed the day after my surgery.

She must be deaf, because she never flinches when my foul mouth runs off as I get back in bed hating life. I think it's the dogs she stays for. She probably feels sorry for Boomer and Brady. And weeks later, during my recovery, it's easy to see the bond the three have formed. Won't they be sad tomorrow when she's gone? It's her last day since I'll be cleared to drive. After my ACL repair and recovery, I'm finally ready to begin physical therapy.

Rita scares me. One afternoon she threatened if I threw any more plates on the floor she would beat me with the broom she was holding. That shut me up real fast. Now she's driving me to my PT session, and that frightens me even more. Her speedy turns that feel like we are tipping on two-wheels have me pressing my imaginary brake, wondering if we'll make it there alive.

"Where'd you learn to drive again?" I ask for the millionth time.

"Why?" She looks innocent.

"You're scary. You'd make a fighter pilot sweat bullets."

"Good. I hope you sweat a lot."

That was the extent of our conversation. I'm sure she's had more than her fill of me already, too.

Now I just keep my mouth shut and eyes closed, praying we'll make it to my destination in one piece.

7

Sitting in the waiting room, I've finally finished filling out all the crazy paperwork for my appointment when a voice with a familiar ring to it calls my name.

"Mr. Wilde."

Struggling to stand, I hobble toward the back, taking great care on my newly repaired ACL, ready to be put through the ringer. No one has to tell me how grueling this is going to be. My focus is on my feet, so I don't pay much attention to the blonde-haired therapist until she stops and spins around.

"Hello, Fletcher."

What the fuck! My head snaps up in disbelief. Almond-shaped hazel eyes, the very same ones I used to get lost in for hours at a time, peer at me beneath a feathering of thick lashes. Her gaze takes a lazy trip up and down the length of me, scrutinizing me as though I were an insect, or some other undesirable life form. I get the distinct feeling if she were taller than her five foot seven inches, she would be staring down her cute little nose at me in a haughty manner. Even still, she is every bit as gorgeous as she was the first day I saw her in high school. Scratch that. She's better—more mature in a refined way. But as usual, it's her pouty-lipped mouth that holds my attention the longest. Images of what that mouth can do—wait! What the hell am I thinking? "No. This isn't going to work."

A smirk appears on that gorgeous face of hers. The one I used to be so in love with. The one I thought I was going to spend the rest of my life with.

"Fine. Feel free to see someone else. Let me warn you, though. We only have one other therapist in this office, and he only works half-days every other Thursday. So good luck with that. Unless you want to drive all the way to and from Asheville every day."

Then she has the nerve to wink at me. And all I can think about is her dumping me. *Bitch*.

CASSIDY

He did not just call me a bitch. I stomp into the private office we use for consultations, only Jenny is there with her lunch.

"Tell me that's not Fletcher Wilde."

"It is." Though I'm not sure how the word escaped my mouth, considering I was grinding my teeth.

"Oh my God, oh my God. I have to meet him," she says while waving her hands wildly in the air.

"Yeah, you should run along. He's probably at the front waiting to reschedule his appointment with Cory." She stares at me, waiting for me to say more. I throw a thumb over my shoulder in the direction of the door. "Hurry or he'll just leave."

She runs from the room with a confused but wide smile on her face. I sit in the chair to catch my breath. When I saw the name on the schedule, I'd assumed it was his father who needed help. I had no idea he'd come back to town.

Why now after all this time? He made his choice when he left, and I'd made mine. We'd tried the long distance thing, and it failed epically.

"Cass." I glance up to see Jenny in the doorway. "He hasn't left. He's still waiting for you in room two."

Her eyes don't meet mine, and I know she's got a crush. Who wouldn't? He's fucking beautiful, but a total fucking asswipe. I don't have time to kill her hero worship for him. Maybe he's into eighteen-year-old girls these days.

"I'll be there in a minute."

She gets her food and leaves for the breakroom, which is where she should have eaten in the first place.

Before I go back, I text my friend Gina, *The prick has arrived.*

I take in a deep breath and walk into the room. Fletcher is sitting in the chair, which makes him look so goddamn helpless, and I half-forgive him in my head.

"So, Mr. Wilde, I hear you approve of my services," I say, as I take in his thick brown hair and golden brown eyes. The sheer size of him makes me feel small when I'm this close to him. But I remember how those arms of his would wrap me up and make me feel safe.

"Cass," he says, breaking me out of the spell he's cast. "Don't give me shit, okay? I just got a call from my agent that I might be cut from the team if my prognosis isn't good."

Cass. Only he called me that. More memories of

stolen kisses and hot nights in a confined car bombard me. Then in college, when we had to sneak around to get naked, risking a roommate showing up at any time. That only makes my chest hurt as I remember watching him walk away from me that last time.

"Let's keep this professional, Mr. Wilde. You can call me Mrs. Miller from now on."

"Married, huh? No wonder I didn't recognize the name."

I don't bother to respond to his comment.

"Look, I'm booked today. We've already lost time. Either you play by the rules, something you know all too well, or you can make an appointment with my colleague. I'm sure he can see you in a couple of weeks."

Shocked, his mouth opens before he closes it. His jaw works a few seconds before he grits out, "Fine."

For a second, I'm gripped again with pain that he'd rather wait and see someone else before I pull myself together. *Remember professional.* "Okay, I'll have Jenny set you up with another appointment."

"Cass—" When I glare at him, he amends his word. "Mrs. Miller, what I meant was, let's get this show on the road, because I have to be on the field for the season opener."

It's Ms. Miller, but I don't correct him. Instead, I contemplate telling him his odds of making it on the field won't be good unless he works his ass off. But, I decide we've had enough confrontation.

"If you'll take off all your clothes except your

underwear and cover with this." I reach inside a drawer and hand him the paper gown. "We'll get started on electro stimulation."

"What? Fuck, Cass, you know I don't wear underwear."

"Mr. Wilde, I'm not sure what you do these days, but if you aren't wearing any undergarments, we can work on your shoulder and lower back. Leave your pants on. But remember this for next time."

"How is this going to get me on the field?"

Sighing, I try to remain calm and patient. He isn't the first to question our methods.

"Although I have some leeway, this is what your doctor has prescribed for you. The type of injuries you suffered need time to heal. We are working on pain and muscle stimulation. There would have been a massage if you hadn't wasted most of our allotted time."

I see his smirk and ignore it.

"I'll be back in a few minutes," I add before leaving the room.

Pacing in the office, I try to cool down because, dammit, I remember he goes commando. Heat licks up my spine with the memory. The guy was good with his hands, not to mention everything else.

Thankfully, he kept his pants on, and I apply all the tabs that will send the twenty second electric burst in certain areas with a five second pause in between. I'm not sure who's getting more electrical stimulation—him or me.

Because I only have to work on his upper body, I give him a massage. And, damn, if touching his shoulder doesn't make me wet. What the hell am I going to do in a couple of days when he returns for the full deal?

By the time he leaves, I'm more relieved than I care to admit. I have to cool off, so I stand outside in the crisp air to help clear my mind. He'd been my heart and soul. When he made the decision to leave the university a year early for the NFL draft, that started the slow spiral to our relationship unraveling. He'd asked me to leave with him. Transferring would have been easy, but my dad had been ill and I couldn't move halfway across the country and leave him alone. When Fletcher went to spring training, I'd been supportive and trusted him with my heart and soul. However, the media game they made him play was hard to watch and swallow, especially when he was too busy to talk and explain about the women and groupies that were always near or on his arm. It left us arguing until our relationship finally broke because of it.

Seeing him now makes me rub at the ache where my heart still hurts from him walking away. Unfortunately, I'm also reminded of how a look from him gets my blood boiling for more carnal things like no other man has. Why Fletcher Wilde still has that damn effect on me, I don't know. And I wish he didn't.

FLETCHER

What the hell is Cassidy doing here? I thought she'd moved to—hell, I don't know where. After we split, I stopped trying to figure out where she was because it was too much of a reminder of what we had ... of what I'd lost. Fuck me! How am I going to get through this? Having those perfect hands of hers massaging my muscles? Touching my skin? Jesus fuck. I'll be lucky if I don't shoot off all over the fucking place. Fuck, fuck, fuck! Note to self: jack off before PT every day. At least twice.

"What are you groaning about?" Rita asks.

"I'm not groaning."

"Yes, you are. I know a groan when I hear one. Usually you growl, but that was a groan. Maybe even a moan."

"Never mind that. Pay attention to the road and watch your speed."

And for that comment, she hits the gas and takes off like she robbed a bank and the cops are chasing her.

"What's your hurry?" I ask, grabbing the door handle. She knows I hate it when she drives like this.

"I want to get out of this car with you. You're nothing but a grump."

No point in arguing with the truth. We get home in record time. She's going to need new tires after this. Though, with what I've been paying her, she'll be able to buy a new car. She stomps into the house, not offering to give me a hand. Oh well, it'll be good practice for me since I'll be on my own tomorrow.

At her usual time, Rita packs up her stuff. I do find the words to thank her. She's gone beyond what a normal person would do for me, and I tell her.

"Stick it up your behind, Mr. Wilde. It's your money that kept me here. Oh, and the dogs. Good-bye, Brady and Boomer. I'll miss you. Bite him in the ass when you can."

And that's it. She walks out without another word. I deserve no less. I should feel remorse, but I'm too deep into my self-pity for that. Maybe when I'm over all this, I'll write her a nice note and send her some flowers. Women love that stupid shit. But right now, I limp on over to my favorite piece of furniture—the liquor cabinet—and pour myself some Jameson. Lying back in Dad's recliner, the one Mom wants to ditch, I now see why he loves it so much. Drink in hand, Boomer and Brady by my side, I watch a little TV and wonder what would've happened if Cass and I had never broken up. And when I try to remember exactly what happened between us, I can't pinpoint the cause of the breakup.

"She should've been mine, guys. I never should've fumbled that one."

Brady must agree because he lets out a huge whine that sounds similar to *dumb ass*.

All night, the only thing I can think of is *her*. Her hair, her eyes, her smile, and her voice. My next therapy session can't come soon enough. It sucks she's married. Still, I'm going to make the most of my time with her, like I did when we were in high school. That is, if she'll even respond to me verbally. From all indications, she hates my guts as much as Rita does. And maybe by the end, we can at least be friends.

I show up at my appointment, prepared to strip off my sweats.

"Hello, Fletcher." She enunciates each syllable succinctly. "Did you wear your panties today?" Her snarky voice comes to me from across the waiting room. I'm ready to rip her a new one for saying that in front of everyone when I notice the room is empty, save the two of us.

"I guess you can't wait to find out, can you? Have you been dreaming about me, Cassidy? How does your husband feel about that?" I can't help the little taunt I fire back at her.

Her lips pinch together, and I know I've hit a nerve. Serves her right, trying to embarrass me like that. But, damn, if she doesn't look sexy as I watch her bite her lip. *Fuck, she's married, Fletch.*

Grabbing my crutch, and I hate that little motherfucker, I walk with as much dignity as one who is in as bad of shape that I am into the therapy room.

"Strip," she spits out.

"Happy to." I yank my pants down, and much to her surprise, I'm wearing shorts underneath. "Disappointed?" I purr.

Her eyes bounce up to mine and back down to my … aha! She's checking out my goods! That man of hers must not be taking care of business.

"Don't worry. Things are fine down there. In fact, they've improved since you've seen them. Care to take a look?" *Bad, Fletcher, she's taken.* But I can't seem to stop myself.

Everything from the bottom of her neck to the tips of her ears brightens to a nice shade of fuchsia.

"Asshole," she mutters. "Sit down and stop wasting my time."

I sit, and she asks me a bunch of questions and starts doing shit to my knee that has me gritting my teeth in no time. Sweat beads on my forehead, and I grip the table I'm sitting on, hoping I don't squeeze the plastic cushion thingy into smithereens.

"How you doin' there, Fletch?"

"Fine," I pant. She knows perfectly well how I'm doing. This shit is killing me.

She finally releases that leg, and I want to say a prayer to God above for saving me. That was worse than getting hit by the car. She leaves and quickly returns with one of those ice wraps, and soon my knee is cooling down and feeling better.

"Now for your shoulder."

"Look, can you do me a favor? Try not to damage me any more than I already am."

She stops for a minute and lays a long hard look on me. "I would never injure you. I'm here to help you."

Harrumph. "Sure didn't feel like it."

"This is not about feeling good. It's about getting you better," she says.

Our eyes meet, and for the first time, there's a possibility I might detect a bit of compassion in hers. It could be we've reached somewhat of a truce.

CASSIDY

Perhaps it is my familiarity with him that I choose to reach over to pick up the chart behind him instead of taking the long walk around.

"Damn, Cass, any guy that gets this close can see down your shirt."

His words breeze between my breasts, and I go rigid in order to stop myself from shivering.

Quickly, I straighten and take a step back as I glare at him. "It's really none of your business who sees what's on me, is it? And I thought I told you not to call me Cass."

He lifts his chin before he lets it fall in defeat. "You're right. I'm sorry. And not just about—"

"Don't," I warn. "We are not here to rehash the past."

"It's just—"

"Dammit, Fletcher, let's just get this out of the way. I *loved* you. I thought you loved me. But you chose football as your first love. I was devastated, but I got over it. So leave it in the past. Right now, I'm here to get you back to your beloved game. And that's my job and what I plan to do."

His lips thin, and it takes me a second before I look away from them. The rest of the appointment is awkward, but we muddle through it.

When he leaves the office, I feel like I can breathe at last, and the heat dissipates from the room. Once the day is finally over, I'm in need of a serious drink because Fletcher's reappearance has unlocked my libido. The damn thing has been on hiatus for months and now wants to assert itself.

"You need a date," Gina says from behind the bar of The Dirty Hammer, where she works.

"I need a drink, and make it a double. And you've already fed me. So don't give me shit."

"He hurt you, Cassie. He broke you, and I had to help you put the pieces together."

"We hurt each other," I admit. "I could have gone—"

"He could have not been like every other man out there either."

"Don't, Gina. As much as I want to hate him, he's a good guy." I nearly choked the words out. "He got caught up in the game."

"Yeah, the game of *follow his dreams, he says*. Forget about yours."

"Let's not go there. Just give me the drink."

She harrumphs. "He's got you all hot and bothered

again." I flip her the bird, but she doesn't see it because she stares toward the door. "Speak of the devil."

I turn to find Fletcher lumbering through the door. Hastily, I swing my head around and pray he doesn't notice me.

He saddles up to the end of the bar nearest the door and calls out, "I have a takeout order to pick up."

There are many places to eat in town, but we used to come here a lot long ago. So it isn't surprising to see him here. The bar has the best wings and fries basket, which is popular when watching the games on the big TVs mounted on the walls.

"Name," Gina says sweetly.

"Cut the crap, Gina. You know damn well who I am." His voice is as gruff as it always is, and it stokes all the hidden places on my body. I squeeze my legs shut.

Gina glances my way, and I look over at the wall and pray again to any god that will hear me that he doesn't see me.

"Would that be under Fletcher or *Fickle* or maybe *Fucknut*?"

His sigh is long-suffering. "I get it. You believe I made a serious *fubar* with your girl, so you're doing your best Rottweiler impression. But I'm having a shit day, and I just want to eat. Can we call a truce?"

Gina eyes him up and down. "I don't know, can we?" She drums her fingers on the counter as if in contemplation. His earnest eyes grow weary as he watches her and hasn't noticed me. At least I don't think he has. "Actually, we can't. We don't serve fuckers like you here."

My bestie isn't budging, and I decide to give him a pass and out myself.

"Gina, get the guy his food."

She rolls her eyes in my direction, before rolling them again. "Fine. Give me a minute."

"Thank you," he says. But it wasn't clear exactly who he was saying it to.

Gina heads to the back where the food is prepared. I turn away, toward one of the TVs mounted on the opposite wall, and pretend to watch baseball.

It's not late, yet I'm not surprised when the door opens and a man drunkenly stumbles into the bar. The once beautiful man with bright eyes and big dreams looks disheveled and unshaven in the most undignified way.

"There you are," he announces, stabbing a finger in my direction.

Mentally I count to three while I load my lungs with some calming air. I don't want to have a knock-down, drag-out argument with my ex here, especially with Fletcher to witness my shame.

"Calvin," I say when he gets close.

"Cassidy," he mocks as if I'd said his name like a curse. And maybe I had.

"Why are you here? You're drunk, and you shouldn't be driving."

"It's a free world, and I'm here because you owe

me."

My jaw aches as I grind my teeth together. "I don't owe you anything. You took everything and left me with a bunch of bills I'm still paying off."

So far our conversation has been halfway civil. No yelling, not yet at least. Of course, that thought comes a moment too soon.

"You still owe me for the house."

"The house is mine. You know this. It states it in our settlement."

"I want my share when you sell it."

There really wasn't a reason to answer him, as we've had this conversation several times since the divorce, but I do anyway. "I haven't sold it. And I don't plan to anytime soon."

"That's not fair. I need the money."

A different voice enters the mix. "Is there a problem?"

Calvin has to look up to see Fletcher looming over him. That doesn't stop the fool. He's too drunk and too stupid to care he could never win a fight if it comes down to that.

"I'm talking to my wife, so buzz off."

Fletcher's eyes flick to mine, and I sigh. He's going to find out soon enough anyway.

I say to Calvin, "I'm not your wife, nor have I been for over a year. Just leave, and take a cab."

"Don't you worry about me, Cassie, unless you want me to give you a ride for old time's sake? Word has it you've been keeping those pretty legs of yours closed tight."

What the hell? Is he keeping tabs on me? A bonfire rages in my cheeks.

"I think it's time for you to leave," Fletcher warns.

Out of the corner of my eyes, I see Gina approach. "It is time for you to leave, Calvin. You know I can't serve you."

"Two bitches and Paul Bunyan. You all can fuck yourselves."

He makes his way for the door, and I mutter to no one, "I hope he's not driving." Because despite it all, I don't want him to get hurt. Somewhere in there was the man I thought I loved or at least cared deeply about at one point in my life.

"He's not," Gina says, answering my question. Her eyes are glued to the front window.

Idling at the curb is a car all too familiar to me. It belongs to Calvin's trashy girlfriend he'd cheated on me with. Apparently, she's supported him through his joblessness. Not financially, that had been me. I'd nagged him too much to find a job, so he found her instead. That was his excuse at least. His unemployment checks must have run out and now he is back to bothering me.

"Here's your food." Gina hands a bag to Fletcher while maintaining her scowl.

My bestie stands in as the line drawn in the sand between me and all my bad mistakes.

Fletcher glances at me, but I look away. "Here, keep the change," he says to Gina before limping off.

After the door closes behind him, she says, "Seriously, girl, you and I need to have ourselves a night on the town."

"Can I get that drink?"

She gives me the saddest smile which mirrors my inner turmoil. I certainly know how to pick 'em.

Only before I get my drink, Fletcher comes back in spouting curses like a man who stepped in dog shit.

"Gina!" he shouts. Her eyes narrow, and I wonder what's crawled up his ass in a short time.

Pushing locks that are midnight black from her face, her glare pins me as she stomps over to him.

"Yes."

The word is clipped, and if Fletcher knows what is coming he'd back down from the mad he's sporting.

His fist hits the bar top. "Do you have the number to the garage the..."

"Wilson's," Gina finishes for him.

"Yeah, the Wilson's still run it?"

She nods. "I do. But," she eyes the clock over the bar, "they should be closing for the day."

"Closing? What the fuck is wrong with this town? Give me the number anyway."

Gina eyes me, and I nod. He'd been kind of cute coming to my rescue with Calvin. Gina glares at me but rattles off the number anyway. Cars break down all the time in town. Most folks don't own brand new ones, so

26

everyone knows the number for the garage.

Fletcher is a big guy with deep lungs and his voice carries as he speaks into the phone. "What? I need a tow. No, it can't wait until fucking tomorrow. Wait, I'll pay—"

He stares at the phone, and I know he's been cut off.

"Goddamn townies."

"You know what—" Gina begins.

I let out a sigh resigned to what I have to do. Walking over from my spot, I stand in front of my first love. "I know it's been a while, but things move slowly here. Troy is never going to come for your truck now. I'll give you a ride home and sweet talk him tomorrow into forgiving your shits of the mouth."

"Shits of the mouth?"

Goddamn, if he doesn't look so cute perplexed.

"Come on, Fletch. Let's go."

"What about my truck?"

"You can sleep with your truck and make babies for all I care. But if you want to get home, you're going to have to part ways with her for the night and catch a ride home with me."

He's had that truck since high school. I don't understand why he still has it, but I don't wait for his answer. I prowl out into the growing dusk, and he follows way too close. Any closer and my clothes would erupt in flames. *Damn him.*

"This is your car."

I'm not sure if he's annoyed or amused.

"I happen to like my Mini Cooper. It's perfectly suited for me."

"And how am I supposed to get in there?"

I shrug. "I can always ask Gina for some rope and strap you to the hood."

His eyes narrow. I click the unlock button.

"Come on. I know for a fact a guy your size can get in the car. Plus, you're lucky I'm not giving you shit for walking around without your crutches."

My father is a tall and solidly built man, and I've driven him around with no problem.

"I didn't have that far to go, so I left the crutches at home." He pauses in thought before glancing back at the bar. "Maybe I can get a ride from Gina."

A frosted laugh puffs out of my mouth. "Now that I want to see." When he eyes me with confusion, I add, "Gina rides a Harley."

He stares at me in disbelief. "In this weather?"

"What can I tell you? She's a badass. Plus, she lives upstairs over the bar."

"Maybe I'll just call Mark."

Mark is Fletcher's best friend.

"I heard he moved to Asheville. That's thirty minutes away. Stop acting like a grumpy old man and just get in the car."

I open the door and hold out a hand. He resentfully takes it. It's almost comical how low he has to bend before he tries to fold himself into the seat. As funny as

28

it is, I make sure he doesn't put undue stress on his leg.

"I can't move the seat back. Where's the button?" he complains.

His one leg is still outside of the car, and I have to lean over and in between his legs to reach under the seat.

"Sorry, Fletch," I say begrudgingly. "We're all not rich like you. I could only afford the base model, so you'll have to remember how to push the seat back."

His hand lands on the back of my head. "I have the sweetest memories of you positioned like this."

When I yank my head up to glare at him, I bang the crap out of it under the console.

"Dammit," I spew, as he continues to smirk at me.

I'm stuck between wanting to hurt him and not wanting to because of my job. His hand covers mine as I feel for the goose egg surely there. His eyes soften on mine, and I stare at him a moment to long until a gust of wind reminds me it's not summer. I pull back out of the car, losing contact with him. I focus on his leg and gently help him get his braced knee into the car. Watching him contort into a pretzel lightens my mood. I do my best to suppress a laugh before I close the car door. He says nothing, but he's lost the smirk in favor of a one-sided curl to his lip in a snarl that says more than enough.

When I turn on the car, Shania Twain blasts through the speakers as if she were pulling out the words from my head. It was something about what doesn't keep her warm in the middle of the night.

The drive isn't that long, and the song ends just as I pull up to the remarkable farmhouse. It's always been the envy of everyone in town. It's a stately looking two-story farmhouse with a wrap-around porch and many windows to let in light.

"Nothing ever did impress you," Fletcher murmurs.

The temperature in the car takes a nosedive, and it has nothing to do with the air outside. Therefore, watching him uncurl himself from my car isn't as funny as it should have been.

"Thanks," he mutters once he's out.

The door shuts, and I feel like I should say something. In fact, when he stumbles, I jet out of the car, realizing my mistake for not helping him out in the first place. But I'd been lost in his big brown eyes, which looked so innocent when I knew differently.

"Are you okay?"

He glares at me. "I would have been better off walking home."

When he rubs at his knee, I tuck myself under his arm and help support his weight. Together, we make it to the house. Once inside, I'm hit with a wave of memories.

"I can do it." He tries to shrug me off.

"Where are you headed?" I ask, remaining as stubborn as he is. If he's going upstairs, I'm going to help him get there. I can't have the big guy fall and rupture his knee again on my watch.

"Now?" After I nod, he says, "I'd planned to eat, but

that's not in the cards anymore, is it?" When I don't respond, he continues, "I'm going upstairs to take a hot bath and hope that my knee loosens up. If you're not planning to play nurse and give me a sponge bath, you can go. You've done enough."

"Play nurse? You either sound five and I'm past playing doctor or you're eighty and need a nursing home." He just glares at me. "Besides, I'm sure one of your millions of groupies you have on social media would love to play nurse with you."

FLETCHER

One thing hasn't changed—Cassie's ability to give me a snarky response. Instead of it pissing me off, it does the opposite. I find myself reminiscing about our days back when and how she used to make me laugh. I must have a goofy grin on my face because of her next question.

"You think that's funny? That I'm joking?"

"Not at all. I happen to like your spunk."

"*Spunk?* I basically tell you to get your groupies to help you out, and you like that?"

Rolling my good shoulder back, I lift it a little. "What can I say? I missed that about you." I head up the stairs, one by one, because there's nothing left to add.

When I'm midway up the flight, she says, "Hey, you need some ice, too."

I don't bother turning around. "You know where the freezer is. The baggies are in the drawer right where they always were."

The large whirlpool tub that Mom insisted on adding upstairs is at the end of the hall. At this point, I don't give a shit if Cass sees me naked. My luck—what luck? There is no such thing for me anymore. She can deal with it or not. I don't really give a fuck at this point. The chances of her staying are slim either way. One thing I know for sure now is that she's just as unattached as I am. And that thought warms me more than the water I fill the tub with. As I strip to my skivvies, my knee aches like a motherfucker. I take a seat and wait for the water level to reach the point where the jets can be turned on.

Footsteps precede her voice. "Fletcher, you need to—"

She's not looking at my face. Or my chest. Or my shoulder for that matter. Her gaze is targeted on what lies between my legs. And, dammit, that stupid fucker decides to betray me and stiffens to poke his head out of the water in order to stare back at her. One-eyed fuck. He and I are going to have a little chat after she leaves. Or maybe some hand-to-hand combat. First, I have to deal with her.

"What do I need, Cass?"

"Uh, yeah … uh," she swallows, "you need to ice."

She's still not looking at my face as I say, "Hey, will you look at me for one minute? Unless you want to take a ride. Someone would be more than happy to give you one." *Traitor*.

"Huh?"

"Christ. When was the last time you got laid?"

33

That gets her attention.

"That is none of your business. When was the last time *you* got laid?" Her voice takes on a snappy tone as she throws my question back at me. But at least her attention is off my goods. Maybe the little fucker will lie back down like a good boy. The truth is, I haven't gotten any action in far too long, but she doesn't need to know that. There haven't been many since her because the few I did have never came close to what stands before me at the present time.

"Can we start from scratch? Like this whole night?" I ask.

"What do you mean?"

A frustrated sigh leaves me. "I don't want it to be like this between us."

I expect a snappy response, but that's not what I get. "I don't really either. But after you dumped me—"

What is she saying? "I didn't dump you. I had to leave to go with the pros."

She looks at me like she wants to say *duh*.

"Yeah, you dumped me for the pros."

My hand drives through my hair. "That's not how it went. I had to leave, and you were supposed to come."

That one word has me harder than I thought possible. She speaks, but I'm barely coherent to what she's saying.

"I had to finish college. Then there was PT school, my dad, and I couldn't possibly go."

Reaching out, I take her wrist and pull her closer.

Her eyes widen, making her look like a doe in the middle of the road. And, damn, if that doesn't make her my prey.

The words crawl out of my mouth like a growl. "Take your clothes off and get in this tub with me." I shut off the water and push the button to get the jets running. This is a dead-end conversation, like it will always be.

Her head shakes, sending all that hair I want to wrap around my hand flying.

"You're crazy."

"Maybe." I haven't let go of her wrist, determined to convince her to stay. "Everyone's entitled to a little crazy. Why'd your marriage break up?"

She pins her lower lip under the top one, looking unsure of how she should answer.

"He cheated on me." Her words are soft, but I hear them well enough.

Splashing the water around, I ask, "Is that the only reason?"

When she doesn't answer, I give her hand a slight tug. "Take your clothes off, Cass, and get in here."

"I might hurt your knee."

"Chicken." I splash her with some water.

She jumps back, and I lose my hold on her. "Fletcher, you got me wet."

Her eyes narrow as my grin widens. "That's the idea."

She shakes her head and half-smirks. "Fletcher, we

haven't been with each other in, how long?"

"Too long, but not long enough for me to forget what we had." The words slip out before I can catch them and cram them back into my mouth. I had meant to say it was since draft day when I ultimately changed the course of our lives. She had to stay—her father was sick at the time and things weren't looking good. She didn't want to be that far away from him. Then, when things settled down, and she graduated, she waffled because Oklahoma was halfway across the country. That's when the arguing began. I naïvely thought we could work through it, but things escalated, and ugly words were exchanged. Things were said neither of us most likely didn't mean—at least that was true in my case. Finally, I ended up losing the best thing that ever happened to me. At the time, I thought it was football. I was dead to rights wrong. But when I figured it all out, she had moved on and wouldn't even speak to me. And I couldn't blame her. We both chose different paths.

Eyes like heated caramel striated with moss green and swirled with milk chocolate melt the frost that's held my heart prisoner for all these years. I'm not sure which one of us is more surprised when she drops her jacket on the floor. Her sweater follows, then her jeans. All that remains are her bra and thong. She looks like my best dream, the one I have when I've over imbibed. I'd pinch myself if it didn't make me look like a moron. And she already thinks I'm one so I don't need to give her more reminders.

"Jesus, Cass, you ..." I have to swallow because I'm afraid I'll drool if I don't. "You are so beautiful."

She reaches behind her and the bra slides off her arms, falling to the floor. Her tits are better than I remember. Full and begging for my mouth. I want to suck the hell out of them, but I'm sidetracked when the tips of her fingers tuck under the elastic of her panties and tug them down her long, luscious legs. She steps over the tub and kneels between my legs.

"Are you sure you don't want to eat your dinner?" she asks.

"Oh, I'm going to eat all right. It's just not going to be chicken wings and French fries tonight."

My hands cup her face, and I pull her toward me. When she's an inch from my mouth, all I can think of is how much I've missed this. "I can't wait to taste that pretty mouth of yours. I've waited too long for this."

One thing I don't expect is Cassie's sexual hunger. She's every bit as eager as me, and it surprises us both. The kiss explodes as we crash into each other. Initially, our movements are clumsy, teeth clashing and lips bruising. But then, things become more attuned as we explore and reacquaint ourselves with what we'd lost. Hasty becomes languid; clumsy becomes adept, until we are both lusting for each other and for precious oxygen. It's gotten to the point where I want to seat her on my damn cock, because if I don't do something soon, I'm going to look like I'm fourteen. But I need to get her ready first. And there's a slight problem. I can't lift her up because I only have one shoulder, and I can't kneel because of my fucking leg.

My little savior rescues me. She slides up on the side and asks, "You did say you wanted dinner, didn't you?"

"Are you a mind reader?"

"What do you mean?"

"I was trying to figure out how I was going to do this with one bad shoulder and one bad knee."

"Yeah, I figured you needed a plan."

Staring me in the face, well almost, is her smooth as silk pussy. I don't need another invitation before my mouth hits the goal. I carefully drape her leg over my sore shoulder, and my tongue does exactly what I remember we both love. I bury it inside her and run it around her clit, over and over, until her legs tighten around me. She makes the sweetest sounds when she comes, and, damn, I've missed that.

"Your pussy is so pretty, all pink and glistening." Now I have to tell her the bad news. "I hate to break this to you, but my condoms are downstairs."

"I'm on the pill."

"You trust me? With all my groupies?"

Her eyes widen, and I'm sure I've ruined the moment. But it has to be thrown out there.

"How many, Fletcher?"

"Honestly?" She nods. "Three," I admit. "But none in a while."

Her lips move together as though she's forming a W. Then she says, "I don't understand. The media."

I offer her a sad smile. "I suppose you believe everything the media throws at you. They want me to be *that guy*. I'm not. Never have been."

She slides off the side and into the water. "You get tested, right?"

"All the time. We have to."

"I was tested after the dipshit I was married to cheated on me. I haven't been with anyone else." Her arms wind around my neck, and she kisses me. "I want you, Fletcher."

Then she's moving. Her hips situate above me. We stare at each other while she slides down the length of my cock, slowly but surely. It must have truly been a long time for her because she's as snug as our first time together. And it's damn righteous.

My hands wrap around her ass cheeks, and I commence to lift and lower her to a rhythm that I control. She's tight wrapped around me, and I make sure it's good for her.

"Tell me what you need."

"This," she breathes.

I slide one hand between us to make sure she gets hers because I'm close. Almost too close. I hope this is where it all comes together for her, no pun intended. Once those inner muscles of hers grab my cock and squeeze, I can't hold on any longer. I pump her harder, and my orgasm explodes like a cannon. When she squeezes me dry, I lift my lids to find her staring at me. That's when my nerves fire.

Her soft hand touches my face, and I relax. "Whatever happened with us, Fletch? I thought we had it all and then—"

"I was stupid. Maybe we both were. I didn't read the smoke signals you were sending. My excitement over what was happening overrode everything else, and I just couldn't get why you didn't want to move that far away when it was only a plane ride from here."

"But my dad and school. And then we were like dominos tumbling."

"Yeah, and I didn't understand everything being in the pros entailed. It was eye-opening for sure. But I'm happy to see you got your PT degree."

A rueful smile curves her mouth. "School was important, but I think it was ... never mind. You'll think it's dumb."

Taking her hand, I rub circles on top and say, "No, tell me. I need to know this."

"I was also scared you'd be more attracted to someone else. You know, famous football player and all. And here I was just a small-town girl from the mountains."

And doesn't this make me feel like the biggest piece of shit.

CASSIDY

There is a lot of awkward silence after that. I get out of the tub and try to dry off quickly. I have to help him out, which gives him a chance to snag me before I can run. The weirdness doesn't stop him from finding his way inside me again on top of his bed. And, damn, if I don't let him and ride out the pleasure he offers me.

Later, wide awake with his arms around me, I can see how easy it would be to fall. Fall maybe even harder than the first time. We'd been kids, foolishly thinking we had forever. But we didn't. Now, we're both older and a little wiser. And maybe we're a little more jaded, too.

His even breathing doesn't change when I decide to make a break for it, only to realize his truck is still in town.

Still, I slide out of bed and get dressed. When I open his bedroom door, the dogs are right there in the hall and perk up when they see me.

"Come on, boys," I whisper.

I easily find the dog food, having spent much of my time here over the years. The nostalgia hurts more than it warms my heart. I fill their bowls, not knowing when the last time they ate because Fletcher hadn't fed them when he'd come home. I also give their water bowls a refill. But Boomer, I think it is, wags his tail at the door, so I let him out and step out into the chilly night. Brady follows, or it's the other way around. It's still dark, and I wrap my arms around me, enjoying the bite the night air provides. It gives me more clarity about my dumb choice to sleep with a man I'd loved. I have to work with him, and this will only complicate things.

Not long after, a blanket covers my shoulders, and I crane my neck to see Fletcher.

"I wondered where you went. It's the middle of the night."

The dogs sniff out their spots, and I struggle with what to say. He makes his own conclusions from my silence.

"You were leaving, weren't you?"

No point in denying the truth. I turn and meet his eyes. "Yes, but then I remembered your truck. And the dogs, they needed out."

"Cass, don't deflect. We shared an incredible night, didn't we?"

There is a pleading in his eyes that almost breaks through my bulletproof shell, but I can't afford to have my heart shatter the way it did the last time he left. And he is leaving again.

"We did, but—" He steps back, only to wince. "You should be careful. You don't have your brace on."

"Careful," he huffs. "I don't get you, Cass. You're acting like a dude. You get laid, and then you're heading for the hills. Or maybe I should say the mountains."

The mountains. They are one of the many reasons why we can't be together. I love these mountains and everything in them. Maybe even him, if we could have worked through the distance between us when he left.

"What do you want from me?" I study the wary frown lines on his face. "When we finish with your rehab, you're going back to Oklahoma. My life is here."

His glare turns glacial, and I'm the first to look away, unable to withstand the weight in his eyes. Why had I made that leap? It had been too easy to let my jealousy get the best of me.

"Do whatever you want." He waves a hand, dismissing me. "I'll find a way to town. Go home or wherever you go."

He pivots and limps away. I try to reach out, but he evades me. "Fletch?"

"Go, Cass."

His dismissal stings more than a swarm of bees, but I deserve it. I stand there wanting to cry, but push it back. It's for the best. I have to protect my heart, because it won't survive another break.

My alarm wakes me up early, and I'm disoriented

for a second even though I'm in my bedroom. I still remember Fletcher's skin against mine, and I miss his heat at my back. *Boo me.* I hurry through my morning routine, determined to get to Wilson's when they open at eight.

Thankfully for me, it's my one morning off. Once I strike the bargain with Troy Wilson, I head to Fletcher's because I don't have his phone number, and he didn't answer his parents' house phone. When I drive up, he's sitting on the porch swing watching the dogs play in the front yard. I park and make my way to where he sits.

"Mrs. Miller, I didn't think you made house calls."

Not calling me Cass doesn't go unnoticed. But I'd been the one to want to keep things professional. And I'd been the one to brush him off after he made fabulous love to me.

"I tried to call you, but you didn't answer."

"Oh, that was you with the blocked number."

It wasn't a question. I'd forgotten about that. Calvin had blown up my phone in the early days after our breakup. I had my phone number changed, but didn't want him to have the new one.

"That was me. I wanted to let you know Troy towed your truck." I handed him Troy's business card. "He just needs your key to get working on it."

He started to heave himself up, but I stopped him. "I can get it for you."

Sighing, he says, "They're in my pants pocket. You know where my room is."

His eyes never leave the dogs when he's speaking, and my stomach sours. This is exactly why last night was a big mistake.

"Fletch, I wanted things to be casual with us, not like we are strangers."

His response is sharp and quick. "I don't do casual, Cass. You should know that. And we can't be friends either."

The slap of words is what I need to put things in perspective. I head up to his room and find his pants, determined to get this over with and leave. I pull out the contents of his pocket, which includes his phone. The damn thing buzzes in my hand, and it bobbles. I look down in time to see an incoming text flash on the phone.

M - Hey Fletch. I hear you're in the area. I cheer for the Panthers now. We should hook up soon.

The phone tumbles from my hand, but I manage a great save before it crashes to the hardwood floor. Too bad I can never mention that. I stuff it back into his pocket and march downstairs, my mad growing with each step.

I bang through the door and say, "If you need to get to town, I can drop you off. Otherwise, I can take the keys to Troy. He said he would drive the truck to you when it was done. He figures on a day or two if he has the necessary parts."

Finally, his eyes dare to meet mine, but I look away. He doesn't do casual, my ass.

"I guess I should ask how you got him to change his

mind. What do I owe you for it?"

"You know Troy has always been sweet on me." His eyes roll, and he grumbles something I'm unable to make out.

What he doesn't know is Troy is happily married. His wife is pregnant with their third child and is bedridden for her final month. They've been eating his mom's food, which I understand can peel paint. And an offer of a hot meal had easily gotten him past Mr. McGrumpy's temper on the phone yesterday. I watch his molars grind together with sweet satisfaction.

"Why don't you just drop the keys off then? I wouldn't want to come between the two of you."

I let him think what he wants.

"Fine. If your truck's not ready by your next appointment, I can have Jenny get you or you can reschedule."

"And what do I owe you?" he asks again.

I don't have to think of an answer.

"You can forget last night. We'll be working together for a while rehabbing your knee and shoulder. I don't want things awkward between us."

Left with nothing to say, I spin on my heels and get into my car. Elation and major depression fill me all at the same time. I'd won and lost and am already finding it hard to let go. And worse, he's not even mine.

When I park in my father's drive, I can't help but stare at the house. Fletcher coming home has reminded me how much has changed. The small house with its fading paint still looks the same. Though it looks smaller than it did when I was twelve or even eighteen when I left for college.

I knock on the door before I open it. As much as Dad tells me that I should just come and go as I please, I kind of hope he will have a girlfriend one day.

"Dad?"

"In here."

He's where he always is, perched in a chair with ESPN on his big screen.

"Cassidy, baby."

I go and hug him. Once an imposing man, he's lost too much weight, but I don't say anything.

"Daddy."

"Sit. What's going on? I hear Fletcher's in town."

Of course, he's heard. When I don't say anything, he trudges on.

"You know I always thought you and he—"

"Dad, don't go there."

But he isn't done.

"You've got a big heart. When the guy who had it all left, you picked a fixer-upper who took your all."

"I love you, Dad, but boy talk stopped when I was sixteen."

He lets go of a heavy sigh. "I wish your mother were here. She'd be better at this."

"It's okay. I'm doing fine on my own."

"Are you? You haven't dated anyone. You should be out having fun."

"I do have fun," I snap, feeling petulant.

"Okay, enough of that. Just promise me something. If that boy wants another shot, think about it. And this time, don't say no because of me."

"Dad—"

He holds up his hand. "I know why you didn't go to Oklahoma. And I love you for it. But it's time you live your own life. Besides, I'm better now."

"It's too late for Fletcher and me. Remember, you helped co-sign the loan so that I could buy the practice. How am I supposed to leave now? I'm a business owner."

"True, but happiness isn't something you can buy or own."

Dad's words swirl in my head until Fletcher's next appointment. My hands work nervously as I wonder what seeing him again will feel like. I do know one thing; there isn't a pathway to a relationship for us, not when either of us is willing to move.

When his appointment time comes and goes, I'm at the front desk talking to Jenny.

"Did he call and reschedule?"

There isn't a need to explain who the *he* is. She shakes her head no just as he walks in.

"Sorry, I had a late night and overslept."

Visions of him and the girl labeled M in his phone dance in my head.

I don't bother to say anything snarky in front of Jenny. It would be unprofessional, wouldn't it? I bite my tongue and wait until we're alone in the room.

"We don't have a lot of time, so strip and get into this gown."

He doesn't give me a chance to leave the room. He pulls his shirt over his head and I'm so captivated, I have to swallow. His body is a piece of sculpture that belongs in a museum. I'm so mesmerized, I watch as he drops his pants. He's commando... again. His dick bobs, and a part of me wants to fall on my knees and give thanks to the god of cocks.

Then there is a whoosh, and all the air is expelled from my lungs as he pins me to the door. I hear the lock turn before his lips are warm on mine, and I don't fight it. I kiss him back, dammit, because my lady parts are on fire.

"We don't have a lot of time. My next appointment is in forty minutes," I manage to squeak out.

"I need twenty, and then you can finish me off."

I have no idea what he means, but I'm determined to find out. His hand slides easily into my stretchy yoga pants. Damn, he's not playing fair.

"I want you, but this is the last time," I say before I lose all reason. Because this man is my drug of choice, and detoxing when he leaves will be hell on earth.

FLETCHER

The last time, my ass. This is only the beginning. But she doesn't need to hear that. Instead, I give her what she wants, what she needs. At five feet seven, she's no match for me, so I push her over to the table, the one I usually sit on. In one swift move, she's seated on the thing, and those flimsy stretchy pants are around her ankles. She pushes one leg free, and I spread her thighs, the same ones I've dreamed about for years, and bury my mouth in her pussy. When her fingers sink into my hair and tug my head even closer, I'm pretty fucking sure I've scored a touchdown. Or at least I will in a few minutes.

My tongue goes to town on her clit, back and forth, circling and licking, until she writhes on the table, her ass squirming. The panting spurs me on, so I add some finger action, pumping two of them just so, making sure to hit her G-spot. When her legs virtually put me in a vise grip, I know she's going to come. I have to see her, so I lift my eyes to watch. Her head drops back, and all I want to do is kiss the line of her neck.

As soon as the tiny quivers stop, I move over her and run my tongue from her ear to where her neck and shoulder join. Then, grabbing her calf, I put it around my waist and drive my way to the end zone. A quarterback sneak that leads to a touchdown—that's exactly how it feels. My mouth hovers over hers for a second, and then I kiss her as we fuck. No, I don't feel like this is fucking. With Cass, it was never fucking. It was always making love. Her warm, wet pussy fits around my cock like a tailor-made glove, and she's lightning running through my veins.

"Cass, you're perfect. So damn good."

Her hand wraps around my neck and pulls me in for another kiss. My hips tilt in as she meets my thrusts. We match a prefect rhythm as though we've never skipped all those years. I pull her up into a seated position and reach between us, watching where we're joined. Seeing my dick moving in and out of her is the most incredible sight. My finger touches her clit, and she grabs my shoulder, the good one, as her fingers dig into the muscles.

"I'm going to come again," she says.

"Good. So am I."

When I feel her inner muscles squeezing my cock, I let loose. It's so damn good, I have half a mind to shout out loud, but stop myself right in the nick of time. To let the office know what's going on in here would not be good. Then I lean in to kiss her, but she turns her cheek.

"Don't do this, Cass. You and I ... we're meant to be. You have to feel this." Her legs are still wrapped around me, and when she tries to move, I keep a tight grip on them.

"Fletcher, please."

"You can't run and hide from this."

"I'm not hiding. I'm protecting myself."

"From what?" I ask.

"From having my heart torn to pieces. I can't go through that again."

"Who says you will? And who says my heart came out of that unscathed? You act like it didn't affect me at all. I was devastated by what happened. If it hadn't been for the fact that I had to concentrate so hard on my career, I'm not sure how I would've gotten through it."

Her dubious expression lets me know she's not buying it.

"What?" I ask.

"I saw all the pictures."

"What pictures?"

"Of you with all those girls. They were everywhere. Hanging all over you and you soaking it up like a king," she says. The wounded look in her eyes and the way her shoulders instantly droop tell me all I need to know. Those damn pictures they forced me to take and the places they told me I had to go must've made a terrible impression on her.

"Cass, it was all fake, all for show. That wasn't the

real me. If you would've given me a chance to explain—" My hand slashes through the air. It still pisses me off that I let them have so much control over me back in the early days. It had cost me a great deal.

"Okay, but what about your other options here?"

"My other options?"

"It's not like you owe me an explanation," she says.

"Explanation?" What the hell is she talking about?

"I saw the text," she says. My perplexed expression must show her I need more than this, so she goes on to say, "The cheerleader for the Panthers who texted you?"

"Cheerleader?" I am completely lost now. I don't even know any Panthers' cheerleaders.

Her penetrating gaze is filled with doubt, but then it suddenly hits me. The text I got from Mark. She must've seen it, and I have him in my phone as M.

"Are you talking about Mark?" I watch her bite her lip, realizing she's caught. "Checking my phone, Cass? That's a new low even for you."

"I didn't—"

"Um, yeah, I think you did. How else would you have come to this conclusion, which couldn't be further from the truth?"

She glances at the clock on the wall. "It was an accident. I shouldn't have—" She shakes her head more to herself. "Anyway, I've got to go. It's almost time for my next appointment, and I need to pull myself together."

She unwinds her legs from my hips. She's pulling

away from me and not just physically. "Sure. But this isn't over between us. Tell me you realize that." She's unwilling to meet my gaze, which doesn't bode well for me. However, I'm not going to accept this. I lightly grab her chin between my thumb and forefinger and tip her head back, forcing her to look me square in the eye. "Cass, please. Give us a chance. There is no one, no cheerleader, no fan club. I swear."

"Fletch, I have to think, but I can't right now. I have a job to do. And I have to work on you for a little while."

"Fair enough." I reach for the gown, and she gets dressed.

She has me lie back, and she does some stretching movements with both my knee and shoulder, and then moves into massage therapy.

When she's about ready to wrap things up, she says, "Sorry this was so abbreviated."

"I'm not. In fact, I'd go so far to say I'd like all sessions to be this way." It's impossible to keep the grin off my face. I quickly get dressed.

Before we exit the room, I notice how disheveled she looks so I say, "Hang on." I straighten her hair and wipe the smudge of lipstick off her mouth. "Much better."

She gives me a lopsided grin. "Thanks."

"Do I need to come in tomorrow since I didn't get a full session in today?"

"Yep, I guess you do. See if Jenny can find time to squeeze you in between my appointments."

"Cass, I'll squeeze in wherever you let me."

She purses her lips, but can't stop a smile. We walk back to the front desk, and she says, "Jenny, will you schedule Mr. Wilde for another appointment tomorrow?"

Jenny raises her brows, but doesn't say a word. I leave with an appointment for the next morning, but I also have a mission. It may be a mission impossible, but then, I've never been one to back away from a challenge. In fact, I'm feeling a bit rejuvenated.

Mark's old beater truck is parked outside where I left it. He was kind enough to let me borrow it until mine gets fixed. He came by early this morning with a woman to drop it off. He'd given me a look not to ask, so I hadn't. Besides, I have a goal, and I'm figuring out a way to achieve it. My first stop is The Dirty Hammer where Gina works. Even though it's early, I know they serve lunch, so I'm banking on it being open.

When I walk inside, my eyes have to adjust to the darkness. The place is empty, as it's only eleven o'clock.

A voice calls out from the rear, "Sorry, we're not open yet. That door shouldn't have been unlocked."

"Oh, I'm not here to eat. I was wondering if Gina was in."

The sound of shuffling feet can be heard, and then a man walks up to me. "And who wants to know?"

I hold out my hand saying, "Hi, I'm Fletcher Wilde. I'm an acquaintance of hers."

The guy wipes his hands on his apron before he shakes mine. He's middle-aged with graying hair around his temples, and his reaction makes me wonder if this is Gina's boyfriend or something. "Oh, right. Heard about you from her. Sam O'Reilly."

"Nice to meet you, Sam. Hey, I'm not trying to step in your space or anything."

"Huh?"

"You know. You and Gina." My fingers make a V, and I point them at him.

"Oh, no. We're not … we're just … I'm her boss. Or she's more like mine, if you know what I mean."

I'm pretty sure he's talking about that sassy mouth of hers. I laugh. "Yeah, I know exactly what you're saying. "

He checks out my knee and crutch and asks, "So, how's the recovery going? I pull for the Rockets because of you—you know, hometown boy and all."

"Thanks, man. It's going. That's about all I can say."

"Man, I'm really sorry. You got totally fucked, if you don't mind me saying."

"Nah, I tell it to myself every day. I'm just hoping Cassidy can get me back into shape by some miracle when training camp hits."

"So, Gina?"

"Oh, do you know when I can catch her?"

The dude rubs his whiskered chin for a second. "Listen, she's not due in till five, but I can pull some strings."

"How?"

His head flicks upward. "She lives upstairs, but don't

tell her I told you."

When he says that, I remember Cass saying those same words to me. "Gotcha, and thanks, man. I owe ya."

The staircase is a bit like climbing Mt. Kilimanjaro, but I take them one at a time and cross my fingers when I knock on the door.

"Goddammit, Sam, it's my morning off. Go away," a voice comes from the caverns of what lies behind the wooden door.

"It's not Sam."

After a short pause, a cheeky reply hits me. "Goddammit, whoever it is, it's my morning off. Go away."

My mouth curves into a grin. "You mean you're not the least bit interested in finding out who stands on the other side of this door?"

"Not in the least."

"What if I'm the Publisher's Clearing House dude and I have your million dollar check?"

"You don't. Go away." I hear something crash into the door.

"What if I'm the Power Ball guy and I have your check worth twenty-seven million?"

"You aren't. Now get the fuck out of my face."

Then I remember she drives a Harley so I say, "What if I'm Jax Teller and I'm here to give you my patch?"

"Huh?"

"You know. Like on that TV show?" I ask.

"I don't watch TV. Go the fuck away."

Knowing I've run out of options, I lay it on the line. "What if I'm Fletcher and I'm here to enlist your help in getting Cass back because I am now and have always been madly in love with her? I desperately want her back in my life. And I think if she's honest with herself, she wants the same. And I swear to you on my life I will never hurt a single hair on her head."

Dead silence. I don't blame her since I have diarrhea of the mouth. When I'm about to head down the stairs in defeat, I hear the lock click and the door crack open.

She looks like she stepped out of a hurricane as she rubs at the corners of her eyes like I woke her up. Though she's dead serious when she says, "How can I believe you?"

"It's the truth, Gina. I have always loved her. And only her. I've only been with three women since we broke up, and none of them meant a single thing to me other than a bed warmer when needed."

She swings the door open wide and says, "Come in."

I walk through, and before I can open my mouth, she points a finger at me and says, "And not a word about my place or the way I look."

And I can understand why. It looks like there was an all-out battle in here or maybe that hurricane did happen, and it was confined to her place. A chair is overturned, couch cushions are on the floor, an empty liquor bottle sits on the coffee table, and Gina looks like she's been well fucked. It all adds up, the messy hair, swollen lips, not to mention the small hickey on her neck, and her cheeks look abraded from some guy's scruff. I hope she had a great time.

"Not a word," I say, grinning.

"So, you want her back, huh? After how you left her?"

"That's not how it went, and you know it."

She crosses her arms and gives me that *uh-huh* look. "Then tell me your rendition, Fletcher."

"She didn't want to leave because of school and her dad. At the time, I didn't quite understand, but now I do. But when we could've been together, she misunderstood what was happening, all the staged media attention. And I was too green to say no when they pushed me, and I did everything they told me to. She assumed all the pictures were real, and they weren't. The damage was done in her mind, but I didn't know. It was catastrophic for us. And I tucked my tail and went away to lick my wounds. But, Gina, you have to believe me when I tell you this. I've never stopped loving her. It took me years to go through a day without constantly thinking about her."

"But you weren't there when she cried days on end over you. I thought she'd join a nunnery until she met Fuckdud. You left her primed and ready for that piece of shit to pick up where you left off."

Damn. She holds up a hand. "I'm not done. As much as I hate your ass, you're right. There is some part of her that never let go of you." She shakes her head in disgust. "You two. Can you not just figure your shit out once and

59

for all?"

It guts me thinking about Cass in tears. If she'd cried just once back then, I might have given up everything. But she hadn't. She'd come at me with anger or resigned to us parting ways. I'd assumed she was done with me.

"That's why I'm here. I need you to help me."

She points a finger at me. "If she finds out I'm helping you, she'll cut my boobs off. And I mean it, Fletch. She may still have a sweet spot for you, but she's moved on."

"Can you not just give her a few nudges in my direction? Like maybe say how I'm trying or to think about that I might have changed or to maybe give me the benefit of the doubt?"

She finger-combs the snarled nest of her hair, but only manages to make it scarier than it is. "She's gonna want to know why I've changed my mind about you, 'cuz I'll be honest. I've been your worst enemy. I've called you every name in the book since then."

"I get that. You're supposed to because you're her best friend."

"So, how will I explain my reversal? And besides, she says you're a grumpy asshole."

My head falls back as I shut my eyes. Of course, she would think that. Why wouldn't she? My aunt and Rita thought the same. My agent, too, if I'm honest.

"There's a good reason for that. It's because of this." I motion to my knee and then my shoulder. "I haven't been the best of company. That stupid accident really did a number on me, and there's a strong possibility I may be out for an entire season. But what's bad about it is this is my contract year. In the best of circumstances, if I have a so-so year, I could get traded. But if I don't play at all, well, you can figure it out. My agent is going ape shit on my ass to get in playing condition, and so is everyone else. This could be my career-ender. All because of some asshole. I don't mean to be a prick, but this has really sucked for me."

Her eyes soften one degree less than looking at me like I'm prey. "Damn, Fletcher, does Cass know this?"

"She knows I could be cut from the team."

"What did she say?" One eyebrow lifts as she studies me.

"It was on my first visit to her. She didn't seem affected one way or the other about my news. She just wanted to keep it professional."

The other brow shoots up as her eyes pop. "That doesn't sound like my bestie. I question if she heard you or if she was shocked about you being her patient."

"That part doesn't matter. I'm not here for sympathy. I just want her back in my life."

"Then why wait until now? I mean, if that accident hadn't happened, would you be trying to get her back?"

I have to think for a second, which Gina interprets as no. "See, maybe you need to think about this some more."

"I have thought about it. But I'd heard she was married." Though I never told her that. "I thought she'd moved on."

Gina nods, and I think I've won her over. "So we need to persuade her that you're a safe bet," she says, then suddenly her face lights up.

"What?"

"I know you can't do anything, like throw a ball, but I have an idea. Leave all the details up to me. Give me your number, and I'll call you and tell you where you need to be. This is gonna be good, Fletcher."

CASSIDY

My body aches in a good way. Fletcher has always made me crave the next taste of him. We'd been each other's first and had explored every inch of each other. He'd been open to finding out what got me off as much as I had with him. I hadn't known how much I'd settled with Calvin until now.

Today shouldn't suck, but it honestly does. I dress up, not for a date, and head over to the Boys and Girls Club to set up for the Spring Celebration party we have planned for them.

"Cass, you look nice. Do you have a date you didn't tell me about?"

Gina gives me a one arched brow stare.

"No, no date. I never dress up these days, so I thought why not."

She nods. "Let's go unload your car, and I borrowed Sam's truck."

We spend the time setting up the space with snack food and candy. One of the local realtors in town springs for pizza for the kids. I also set up the areas for kids to make art and candy bags for their families. Several store owners on Main Street have donated stuff for the kids to use, like construction paper and other things to decorate with.

"It's going to be good," I say, forcing a smile.

I'm ecstatic for the kids. It's just hard thinking about my failed marriage and all the feelings Fletcher is stirring inside me when I know he'll be leaving weeks from now.

"It's going to be great," Gina says with so much enthusiasm. It makes me feel bitchy that I can't match her excitement.

When the kids start to arrive, everything changes. Their eagerness for being here and having this opportunity takes my mind off my silly problems and gets me in the spirit of things.

"Are you guys ready for a surprise?"

As the kids cheer, I whip around to see Gina at the head of the room with her hands clasped together.

"We have a special visitor today."

I don't have time to piece it together before Fletcher steps around the corner. There must be a lot of football loving parents, because the kids, girls and boys alike, get to their feet and cheer like he is a rock star. Though it could be the bags he and Mark carry with goodies.

Fletcher's face radiates as he puts the bags down.

"Who here is a Panthers fan?"

Mark waves, and so does Gina, but the kids are smarter than that. I know differently. I've heard a few of them talking about the Panthers who'd been in the playoffs this past season. But they aren't stupid to a good thing.

"Okay, who's a Rockets fan?" They jump up and down and wave. "Great, because I've brought some goodies."

The next thing I know, kids are given an opportunity to choose between a jersey or a signed football. He gives the little ones first choice. I watch as he interacts with the kids, and he's such a natural. I shouldn't be surprised. Fletcher has always had a good heart, but to see him in action warms a place in me I thought was frozen over.

When one of the bigger kids gets his turn, I hear him ask, "Are you going to be able to play with that?" He points to Fletcher's leg that's in a brace.

"Not yet, but I'm hoping a certain physical therapist will get me back into shape."

His eyes meet mine, and I feel a flush blossom in my cheeks.

One middle grader with pigtails says, "My dad says it's your contract year, and you might get cut."

Hadn't he mentioned something about that in our first session?

"No football contract is guaranteed," he explains. "That's why it's always good to have a backup plan."

Interesting to hear coming from his mouth. It's one

of the things we argued about when he left school a year early for the draft.

The girl doesn't let up, having more knowledge than her years suggest. "Didn't you quit college for the pros?"

He nods. "It was a risk, but I didn't give up. I took classes off-season, and I have my degree."

My jaw comes unhinged. How had I not known? Then again, I tried my best to tune out everything Fletcher related.

"Don't look so surprised."

I glance up to see Mark. "Surprised about what?"

"Don't play dumb, Cassie. We both know you did a real number on him when you broke it off and married some other guy."

Fish-mouthing a few seconds, I narrow my eyes. "I didn't break it off." When several heads turn my direction, I realize I said that too loud. Quieter, I add, "He left me. He chose his career and his groupies over us. He didn't come back either when the season was over, and he could have. He didn't fight for us. So don't try to put that on me," I say in a stage whisper.

"I've got two more things for each of you," Fletcher says, garnering my attention. "You guys know I put on a weeklong summer camp in Oklahoma. But this year, I'm going to do a camp here in town. And all of you are invited to participate at no cost to your parents." More cheers. "Settle down. I also happen to have tickets for you and your family to a Panthers versus Rockets game next season."

It's over then. The yelling becomes deafening. I look up to see Gina with a smile on her face. Fletcher has apparently won a piece of my bestie over. And if I'm honest, he's done the same with me.

When Fletcher comes over, I hadn't realized Mark had walked away.

"So, what made you come here today?" I ask, curious.

"I've always wanted to give back. And to be honest, I've donated money to charities in town. But since I haven't wanted to come back, I've never had the chance to do it personally."

"Why haven't you wanted to come back?"

"Truth?" I nod. "You. I didn't want to see you happy with anyone else. It would've been too hard."

I bite my lip and glance away. His finger turns my chin to face him. "I didn't say that as an accusation."

Confession time. "Truth is, I have avoided any media coverage of you because I didn't want to learn about you being with someone else either."

His smile is genuine. "Have dinner with me tonight."

Automatically, my head shakes. "It's probably not a good idea."

It's a typical date night. Everyone will be out in pairs, and I don't want to confuse things with us.

"Cass, it's only dinner, and I don't want to eat alone."

That candy cover coating over my heart cracks because he's too goddamn sweet. "Fletch, I can't."

"Fine. I do need to talk to you about something. So, how about takeout at my house? Nothing fancy."

"Why don't you just tell me here?"

It's his turn to shake his head. "This is about the kids." He searches my eyes before he adds, "I don't bite."

A wry smile forms on my lips. "You do, and that's exactly what I'm afraid of."

"No, you're not. You're turned on. I know you, Cass, and I know your body better."

He does, and the truth is, I don't want to be alone tonight either. Dinner at his place will take some of the pressure off.

"Okay, I'll come."

"Of course, you will. How many times is the question?"

I laugh because he's only playing off my poor choice of words.

"I'll meet you at your house to eat, but that's it."

"Eating is only the beginning, baby."

I groan, "No funny business or I'm not co— going to make it over."

Later, when I arrive at his house, I'm still wearing the dress I'd worn earlier. The fact that I spent an hour arguing with myself about my choice in clothing meant I'm in deeper than I want to admit. But changing into pants seemed like a cop-out. And changing into anything else meant I'm putting too much effort into a quick dinner meeting.

"Cass," Fletcher says from the doorway.

My feet come unglued from the ground. I walk up the porch steps and through the open door as he moves aside.

"It smells good."

"I ordered Thai."

"My favorite," I say.

"I know."

I nod. "What do you want to talk about?"

He points to the kitchen. "Let's eat first."

And we do. The food is delicious, but in a tourist town, restaurants don't last unless they get good ratings.

Fletcher sits back and watches me after the meal is done.

"So, what is it?" I ask.

His face turns pensive. He sighs, and something in it alerts me to what's to come.

"My agent informed me that the coaches and everyone else are worried I won't recover in time. They want me to come back and let the team doctors supervise my rehab."

My chair scrapes across the floor as I push to my feet. "Of course. We're just some little hick mountain town with nobody worthy of rehabbing the great Fletcher Wilde."

"And this is why I didn't tell you earlier. I don't want to go back. I want you to help me get where I need to be. Plus, my parents are in Italy supporting my brother. It's bad enough I'm not there. I don't want to leave their house empty for two months."

"I can watch the house and feed the dogs if those are the only reasons you're not going."

He stands to his considerable height and crowds my space. "You obviously didn't hear the first thing I said. I want you to help me, Cass. And I believe in you. Imagine how your career could explode if I get back on the field and tell the world if not for you I wouldn't be there."

It's true. With his endorsement, the practice could benefit from it. And I've put everything I have into it. If it fails, I not only risk my assets but my dad's since he had to co-sign for me after Calvin ruined my credit. And I'm barely making it while paying off the debts Calvin left for me.

"It would mean that we would have to work together outside of my office during my off hours."

He folds his hands across his chest. "I'm up for it if you are. I'll pay you for your time."

As tempting as it is, I say, "I need to think about it."

"Don't take too long, Cass. I need to tell my agent something tomorrow."

"You'll have my answer by then."

And as much as I want to stay and let Fletcher fuck my brains out, I leave, wondering exactly what I'll tell him in the morning.

FLETCHER

Last night Cassidy told me to meet her at the office around noon today. If she can't get me back on the field, we're both fucked. I won't have a chance in hell of negotiating another contract if I can't prove my worth to anyone, not to mention, her career could possibly be ruined if it becomes known that she's the one who failed to rehab me properly.

But then it hits me. Not ruining her career is even more important than getting a contract signed. What does this tell me? Am I so pussy-whipped already that I'm willing to do anything just to make her look good? One thing I do know is she means the world to me, and I want to make her shine like gold.

She opens the door for me and then locks it after I enter. The place is quiet and empty, since it's Sunday. The office isn't open on weekends, so we have the place to ourselves.

"Ready?" she asks.

"As I'll ever be."

"This is going to be intense, Fletcher. I'm going to push you harder than I normally push patients. You're going to have to let me know whether it's good pain or bad. I trust you know the difference, being an athlete."

"I do."

She begins with manipulation and massage, where I grind my molars to prevent me from whining out loud and sounding like some pansy ass. I've barely recovered from that when she sticks her head in front of mine, and with a bright smile asks, "Ready for some strengthening exercises?"

My feeble muscles feel like mush, and she's just taken them and torn each fiber individually, treating them as though they are rubber bands. Well, they aren't, and I've a mind to tell her as much. And now she wants to know what? If I want to lift weights or something? I think she's purposefully trying to be evil, to pay me back for those disgusting media pictures.

Only I have to put my best face forward or she'll know I'm nothing but a whiny ass bastard. "Whatever you say, boss." And I grin as sweetly as I can, even though sweat is gushing out of me like I'm a fucking thundercloud.

"Okay, here." She hands me two of those wide elastic bands and tells me to step inside of them so my ankles and thighs are wrapped in them. And then I go to work doing all sorts of crazy shit. Who knew those thin little pieces of rubber could be so damn torturous? I'm going to melt every single one I can find if I ever get through this. I need a block of wood to bite down on. This shit is like getting sacked by a three hundred pound defensive end over and over. After fifteen minutes of this, I want to call my mom and cry and ask her for my blankie.

"How ya doin' over there?" she calls out from across the room, clipboard in hand.

"Good. Great." Motherfucker. Get me through this.

"Good job, Fletch. Keep going."

I watch her grab a pen from behind her ear and scribble something down. I wonder if it's *bring out the rack, that old medieval torture device, and put Fletcher on it to abuse him some more.*

When I don't think it's possible for me to lift either leg one more time, she says, "Great job. That was awesome. Now for your shoulder."

Shoulder? I have a shoulder?

"Lie down on the table." And she does that muscle-tearing, ripping-out thing she did to my knee. The next thing I know, I'm stretching my arm against some slanted board, cursing everything known and unknown to man. Why the hell did I ever agree to this?

When those stretching motions are over, I think my right arm is ten inches longer than my left. This could be a good thing. If my arm reaches to the ground, it'll definitely be easier to catch that snap. And a Hail Mary will be a breeze. When I look up, she has one of those fucking bands dangling from her fingers. Scratch the Hail

Mary. I'll be praying that instead.

I'm actually pleased to discover the shoulder exercises aren't nearly as bad as the knee. I push my way through, and then she announces it's time for hydrotherapy.

"Hydrotherapy?" I ask.

"Yeah, you know. Water jets. You must have this in your training facility."

"Well, sure, but we're done with the tor— I mean therapy?"

"Was I too hard on you?" she asks, as her brows draw inward.

"No, I was sure we'd go a lot longer."

"Fletch, it's two o'clock."

Two? I thought it was closer to midnight. "Already? Wow, that went by fast."

"Yeah, I don't want you to overdo it."

"Oh, well, in that case, hydrotherapy it is. Lead the way, boss."

We walk to the rear of the facility and enter a room. There's only one giant tub in there and a smaller one, unlike at our training center, where we have tubs of various sizes for different injury locations. Cass proceeds to fill the tub.

"I imagine you know how these work, right?"

"Yeah, I'm familiar with them," I answer.

"Get in and let the water do its trick."

She walks toward the door.

"You're not staying?"

Stopping, she spins around. "I have to chart your progress. I'll be back. You afraid to be alone in here?" she teases, smirking.

"No, I just wanted some company." I pull off my T-shirt and then slide my shorts off. I'm not thinking too much about it, but then when I see her reaction, I'm glad I did it. She should've known I'd be commando. Stepping into the deep tub, I ask, "Care to join me?"

"You know that's not part of this deal," she huffs and stomps out of the room. But I'm not giving up yet.

The water feels great on my knee. My shoulder is much better than I thought it would be. It's the leg that's giving me fits. But even so, I feel myself getting stronger as time goes on. Leaning back against the tub, I sink into the warm water and allow it to work its magic on me. I don't know what it is, but these tubs are amazing.

I must've dozed off because all of a sudden, I hear the *click, click, click* of her heels across the floor, as she gets closer to the tub. I pretend I'm still in my zone, relaxing away the hour.

"Are you a prune yet?"

"Huh?" I shake my head, knocking the sleep out of it.

"Don't you know it's not safe to fall asleep in one of these? You could slip underwater and drown."

I lean over the side of the tub and point my finger at her. "And whose fault would that be? I told you I wanted you to stay to talk with me."

She acts so flustered; maybe I've gone too far. Her hand is close enough to grab so I snag it with my own.

"Cass, don't be upset with me."

"I'm not."

"Yes, you are. I can tell. It's me, remember? I know you better than anyone."

"You only think you do. I've changed since then."

"Maybe, but not that much. The Cassidy I remember still lives inside of you." I release her hand and push myself to my feet. "She's here." I touch her temple. "Here." I touch her cheek. "Here." My fingers press against her lips. "But most importantly, she's here." I lay my hand over her heart, then bend down and my mouth meets hers. There is not a single bit of resistance in her, so I lick the line where her lips meet and she opens for me. Taking that as an invitation, my tongue pushes through, and hers is there waiting for me.

Naked Fletcher is no match for clothed Cassidy, so my hands slide under her sweater, and the satiny texture of her skin has Fletcher, Jr. turning into a greedy son of a bitch. Impatient fingers undo her jeans and tug them down her legs, while she starts to stroke my cock.

"Get in the tub with me, Cass." I lift her sweater up and over her head.

"Fletcher, this is the last time."

"Yeah, you said that before, but okay." *Not in a million years. I'm going to make you love me, baby, if it's the last thing I do.*

She kicks off her shoes, and the jeans follow. I take a seat, and when I see her stepping into the tub, my day is made.

"I don't want you to do anything that involves the use of your right arm or knee. Let me do all the work. You need to let those rest for a while."

"So, what are you saying, Cass?"

"I'm saying I'm going to ride you hard while you watch."

Fuck. Me.

She straddles my hips, her back to me, and situates herself over me, then places my tip at her entrance.

One of my hands grabs her hip and stops her. "Are you ready? Let me check."

"I'm way past ready. I was ready after I worked on your knee."

My brows arch, and I swallow the *what the hell, why didn't you say something?* that almost shoots out of my mouth.

"Then what are you waiting for?"

"You to release the death grip you have on me."

"Oh that. I forgot. Sorry." My fingers ease off, and she lowers herself, inch by slow inch on me until she's fully seated. Christ, she's heaven. But then she tightens her muscles around me in a firm squeeze, and my hands almost white knuckle it on her again.

"Fuck, Cass."

Then the fun takes off when she pumps her hips up and down, and I end up doing my best to join in and match her movements. Both hands hold the sides of the tub as she alternates between slow rocking and fast pumping. My hand moves to where we're joined, and I find her clit to add more spice to the action. She sits flat to my lap and rocks herself until an orgasm hits, and when her inner muscles tighten on me, it doesn't take me long to find my own. It seems like mine goes on and on, only I know it's just my imagination. It's the motion of Cass's body against my own that's creating the sensation.

My hand reaches around her neck and I pull her against me for a kiss. She's eager for my mouth and offers up her own like dessert.

"When you climax, you make the most beautiful sounds I've ever heard."

She pulls away, and it plows into me that my stupid words just broke the spell that was woven between us. Why did I have to say anything? Me and my dumbass mouth.

"I need to get out of here," she says, as she disengages her body from mine.

"Don't go yet."

"Yeah, I need to get dressed."

"I suppose I need to as well."

The water sloshes around as the jets still run, though it is getting cold.

"No, not quite yet. I have one more thing for you on my list."

"Oh yeah? What is it?" I ask.

"You need to take an ice bath for your knee."

"Are you fucking with me?"

"No, Fletcher. I'm not. At all."

She climbs out of the tub and dries off with a towel from the stack on the nearby shelf, then quickly dresses and marches over to the ice machine where she fills a bucket. I watch as she dumps several loads into a tub and adds water. "All ready for you," she announces with a smirk.

My semi-hard dick instantly shrivels into no man's land at the mere thought of getting into that ice-filled hell. Logically, I know it's the best thing for my knee. Realistically, I want to run like hell because this is going to emasculate the shit out of me. But I can't. Instead, I fill my lungs with air, step out of the tub, and inch my way over to the next form of torture she's devised for me. All I can think of is this had better be worth it.

CASSIDY

Fletcher is way too tempting, and my heart melts more each time I'm with him. Thankfully, his rehab is progressing in the right direction. He might be ready on time if we continue to work hard.

"You look happy. What's going on with you, girl? Are you getting some from a certain football player?" Gina winks.

"Can you please not announce it to the whole bar?"

I glance around, and I'm grateful for the dozen or so TVs that have every person captivated.

"Besides, I thought you hated him. You look almost pleased that I might have hooked up with him."

"Might?" One eyebrow arches up.

"Whatever. I'm going home."

"Mmm hmm," she murmurs. "Is he there waiting for you to ride that pony because you are walking like a cowgirl?"

I flip her the bird, which makes her laugh and me,

too, as I head out for home.

"Don't forget dinner tomorrow night," she calls out before I leave.

Tomorrow Fletcher will come in for his regular appointment. We won't have an after hours session. So I planned to spend time with my girl. She hardly has any nights off. And when she does, she's off with one of the many vacationers that pass through. Gina isn't about the long-term. Maybe it's my two failed relationships or it could be because of her parents' epic failed coupling.

After a quick stop to check on my dad, I pull in front of my home. One of the things I gave up on was a garage. It was a dream this house didn't come with. I lock the car without paying attention. By the time I look up, I jolt.

"Calvin?"

"Cassie."

His eyes appear dull, but not inebriated. I glance at the street, but don't notice his car. It's something I generally look for when I come home so I'm never surprised like this.

"Why are you here?"

He sighs. "Isn't it obvious?" He steps into my personal space and alarms go off in my head. Although he isn't normally violent, his erratic behavior of late suggests that anything is possible. "I miss you, and I realize what a mistake I've made."

This isn't the first of such confessions he's tried to make to me. And a part of me wants to believe him, because this isn't the guy I fell for. Maybe he had high hopes for his future when we first met, but isn't that what drives people to be better? He'd been everything I needed after I was so lost from a broken heart. Maybe I'd been blind to the demons that would later consume him. But I want to hope that somewhere inside him a good man still exists.

Shaking my head, I step back, longing for a weapon, but grateful it's not dark.

"What? Is it that guy? Fletcher?" He spits the name from his mouth, and I see rage curling his lip.

My self-defensive training plays in my head. I maneuver one key between my fingers as a potential weapon. Maybe he's not drunk. Maybe he's moved on to other means of getting a high. And that bothers me. Though I can't keep making excuses for him. He's made his choices, and they are bad ones.

"I think if you're honest, you'll admit he's the real reason we aren't together. You were always measuring me up to him."

There is truth in his words, but no way will I admit that to him. He reaches out a hand and cups my cheek. I flinch back on autopilot.

"There's nothing going on between Fletcher and me. I'm rehabbing him because of the accident. And, yes, he's a friend. I grew up with him."

"That's good to know. Then you can give us another shot, and we can use his attraction to you to our benefit."

I take another step back and find the door. "What's

that supposed to mean?"

"Cassie, the only real problem I had in our relationship was money, and, well, the fact that you weren't adventurous enough in the sack. But we can solve that. You give that guy what he wants, and he'll loan you the money we need to be financially stable."

Now I'm sure he's on something. "Wait? What? You want us to get back together. But you're okay with me sleeping with Fletcher so I can get money from him?"

He actually wears a confused expression. "Well, yeah. We can have an open relationship. Love was never our problem. I still love you, Cassie, but I need more. And I can get that from Tara. She's a great lay, but I don't love her."

I want to grind my teeth, but he isn't worth it. "You need to go, Calvin."

"Come on, Cass—"

"Where's your car?"

Besides changing the direction of our conversation, I want to know if he's gotten a new car. I need to be on the lookout for it so I won't be ambushed again.

"I borrowed one because I knew you wouldn't come home if you saw mine."

He's right about that.

"You need to leave, or I'm calling the police."

His arm rises, and I grip the key tighter, prepared to use it if I have to.

He points at me. "You are such a bitch. This is why you'll always be alone."

With that, he darts down to the street and gets into a light blue car. I memorize it. If I see it again, I'll know I need to be cautious.

After a fitful night's sleep, the next day I go through the day with a professional manner.

"Cass," Fletcher says from the table. I glare at him. "Oh, we're back to that now."

"I don't have time for games today."

"Fine. If that's the way you want it, Mrs. Miller."

The moniker stings more than I want to admit. Probably because it reminds me of Calvin telling me in so many words I'll be an old maid.

I work Fletcher hard, putting him through the paces. We concentrate on gaining more mobility on his knee and shoulder. We are so close at times I'm pretty sure I could name the soap he uses. Touching him is like lighting a fire, but I do my best to ignore it.

"I'll see you tomorrow evening. You can do a few reps tonight and tomorrow morning, but don't push it. We want you healthy, not reinjuring the muscle."

"Yes, ma'am," he says, getting dressed in front of me.

Somehow, I manage to keep my eyes on his and not his beautiful body.

"That's all," I say before fleeing the room.

It would be a lie to say I hadn't wanted him to touch me, but I managed to get through it unscathed.

Later that evening, I've swallowed my first drink before I can warm up the seat while I wait for Gina.

"Another drink while you wait for your guest to arrive?"

I nod at the waitress and pull out my phone.

Gina – Sorry sweets. Sam is in a jam and I can't meet you for dinner.

Great. I flag down the waitress. I'm looking for her over my shoulder when a voice stills me.

"Can I join you?"

His voice is rough, and I turn to see Fletcher.

"I was just leaving."

"Why?"

I swallow. Why was I? "Gina stood me up."

"But you're here, and I'm here. Why don't we just share a table together?"

My stomach growls, and I'm glad for the notice that dampens the sound. "Okay, fine. I am hungry."

He sits, and I watch him wedge himself in the booth. And I realize food isn't what I need. Of course, the waitress materializes as soon as Fletcher's here.

"Can I get you something?" she asks.

His eyes barely leave mine, but he's not an ass. "Sure, if you have a to-go bag big enough for my girl."

She seems half-amused and half-annoyed. "No, sorry about that. Anything else?"

Somewhere along the way, she managed to undo a few of the buttons on her shirt, but Fletcher doesn't notice.

"A beer would be great."

After she lists out the IPAs they have, he settles on

one, and she moves on to her quest. I don't bother to ask for the drink I ordered. It's probably best I stay sober.

"So, what brings you here?" I ask coolly. Something about this whole thing feels like a setup.

"I have to eat, and so do you."

I'm about to ask if he and Gina set this up when the waitress comes back with both of our drinks. So she hadn't forgotten. Points for her. He doesn't speak until after she leaves.

"Do you remember the first time I took you out?"

The question is so far from where I'd planned to take the conversation, I'm speechless for a few seconds.

"I remember," he continues. "I was nervous as hell. I had the prettiest girl in school agree to go out with me, and I was certain I'd fuck it up somehow."

"Fletch—"

"And here you are. Still the prettiest woman I've ever laid eyes on, and once again, I'm nervous."

That stops me.

"Why are you nervous?"

"Because I'm afraid you're going to crush my heart all over like you did those years ago."

I practically attack the poor man as I capture his face across the table. Our need for each other isn't for public consumption. He manages to drop money onto the table as we kiss our way out the door. I'm in the seat, frantically tugging at his fly as he puts the truck in gear. And then, I suck my prize in all the way to the back of my throat. I manage to relax so I don't choke myself, but I work out all my frustrations as I give him the best damn blow job one can give while the guy is driving.

The vehicle comes to a stop, and he pulls me free. "I'm close, but I want to finish this off inside you."

Glancing up, I realize we are at my place, which confuses me.

"How did you know where I live?"

It should have creeped me out, but I'm more curious than anything else.

"Mom told me once."

I nod, and he helps me out. I fumble with my keys, and he recovers. He's always had good hands. Once inside, he plasters me to the door, and my purse drops to the floor with a dull thud.

Roughly, he pushes my shirt up, and my breasts pop free from my bra, which is completely useless against him. His fingers work one as his tongue works the other.

He switches, and his hand dips under the fabric that covers my center.

"Wet and always ready for me."

My head bobs as I think how wrong Calvin is. I am more than a missionary style girl; he was just never Fletcher. Therefore, he was right on some things. I'd never given him my full heart. But when Fletcher's two fingers thrust inside me, all thoughts of Calvin disappear.

"I need you now," I groan.

Together, we work at his jeans. He unzips while I hook my fingers in for leverage to push his jeans down. I grab his ass, which is fanfuckingtastic. Then we work off my jeans. We only get one leg completely off before he's hiking me up to wind my legs around him. God, he's the man of steel when he lifts me with his good arm and shoulder. My back glides up the door before he sets me on the sturdy table near the door, and then he's sliding into me.

We groan in unison when we are joined. My insides blaze from the friction we create.

Then, it's my turn to moan out, "I'm close."

"Not yet, baby. Where's your bedroom?"

I point, and he turns. "Why?"

"I'm going to fuck you where you sleep so you don't forget me, not even in your dreams."

My jaw drops, but my mind still works. He helps me to my feet, but I'm wobbly. He may have the bad leg, but I'm the one with the weak knees. "The second door on the left," I squeak in anticipation.

His long strides have us there in no time.

"Purple?" he asks, one brow rises.

I shrug when I hit the mattress with a little bounce.

"On your knees, baby. I know how you like it."

He doesn't let me turn on my own. He flips me over and hooks an arm under me to hike up my ass. And then he pushes inside me, stretching me beyond limit. His fingers work me somewhere north of where he rocks my world. As I scream his name, he pulls out, only to find that other place. It's been far too long since I've done this. Calvin didn't know how. If he'd only known just how adventurous I was with the right man.

"Fuckkkk…" He stills. "Are you okay?"

I can only move my head in the affirmative. "I should be asking you. Maybe I should be on top because of your leg."

"Don't worry about me, baby. My knee is not getting in the way of me having you like this."

His fingers find the magic button between my legs as he pumps inside me. Fletcher is no small man anywhere on his body, and the bite of burn slowly turns to pleasure as he continues to work his way. It doesn't take long before I'm pushing back, wanting him to move faster, and he does. I'm crying out my next orgasm when he loses control and follows me over that cliff.

As we collapse onto the bed, panting, I know for sure I will be dreaming about this man for the rest of my life as my heart takes the leap without me knowing. Although it changes nothing, he's still leaving, and I'm still not going anywhere; I can't help but admit to myself that I'm still in love with him. But love doesn't change that our lives are in two different places. Dad thinks it would be easy for me to leave, but my finances are in the shitter. I can't start over, not yet. And my pride would never allow me to tell Fletcher about my money problems. I won't be one of those women who want to take from him. So I can only cherish what we have now, and hope I'll survive when he leaves.

FLETCHER

Cassidy will be my forever girl if I can only convince her I'm her guy. Stubborn as old Mr. Rafferty's mule and hardheaded as the rock mountain they blasted through to create I-40, it won't be easy. But I'm not going to give up until I win her over. Last night at her house surpassed any of my expectations. Never did I imagine she would allow me to spend the night. Poor Brady and Boomer were bustin' a bladder to go out this morning, and Cass gave me hell about that, too.

"What were you thinking, leaving those poor pups inside all night?"

I don't dare tell her I never thought she'd offer for me to stay over and no way in hell was I turning that invite down. I'll just clean up dog pee if I have to is all there is to it. Or buy new floors for Mom and Dad if it's that bad.

But I don't have too much to be concerned about.

They almost knock me down to get out, though, and I'm pretty sure they pee for ten minutes. Then they kiss me for like a half hour without stopping. Next time Cass is coming home with me.

As I feed the dogs, I think about what we did, what I did to her, and my dick springs back to life. Damn, I'm going to have to temper those thoughts, or I'll walk around with a fucking stiffie all day. And I won't see her again until my appointment this afternoon.

Checking the time, I know it's too early, but I send the text anyway. I'll eat what she dishes out at lunch, after I buy, of course.

A few hours later, I walk into the cute little deli on the outskirts of town, the one I didn't think Cass would come to for lunch because it was too far from her work. My "date" is waiting for me.

"So, how'd it go?" Gina asks.

My mouth has been turned up all day. "Great. Not perfect. But it was awesome."

"You knocked yourself off a piece then, did you?"

"Jeez, Gina, this is Cass you're talking about."

"So? She needs to get laid just like the rest of us. I take it you did my girl good then?"

Shaking my head, I say, "I don't quite know how to answer that."

A sly grin spreads across her face. "You just did. I bet you two got into some kink, didn't you?"

I fish-mouth several times and then look at the white ceiling, trying to think up a clever reply. But she saves me by tapping my arm and saying, "I'm proud of you, Fletch. You're really living up to your name."

"My name?"

"Yeah. The Man with the Hands. Isn't that what they call you?"

"No, it's not." I rub my hand over my head. "They call me Wilde Hands—as in my last name."

She waves a hand and says, "Same difference. I kinda like that. Wilde Hands, huh?" Then she giggles and leans in. "How wild did they get?"

I lean in and say, "You'll have to ask Cass."

"Dang it and she won't tell me a thing."

Her disappointed expression reminds me of a Beagle puppy.

"You're terrible. What's next?"

Both of her hands grip the table as she pushes back. "You mean to tell me she still isn't on board?"

"Like I said before, she won't ever be convinced because she is of the mindset that we're destined to be apart. I have to convince her otherwise, and the only thing I can think of is to figure out a way where we're somehow thrown together."

"I can't fake-stand her up again. She'll figure that out," Gina says.

"Is there a night she usually shows up at the bar?"

"Yeah, on Thursdays, but that's not always a given."

"How about this? Call her Thursday and apologize again and ask her to come in to catch up since you didn't get to last night. I'll show up then."

"I could do that."

"In the meantime, I'll try to come up with something else."

"Sounds good. Now, what are you buying me for lunch?"

"Whatever you want." And I'd get her a new car if that's what it is, as long as I get my girl back.

PT is brutal that day, as it usually is. Cass puts me through hell, but I keep telling myself it's all for a good cause, and it seems to be working. It's hard to believe the improvement in both my knee and shoulder. She really knows her stuff when it comes to sports rehab. Getting back on the playing field by training camp is the goal, but is that cause as good as it once was? Football has been my life for as long as I can remember. I've lived, breathed, slept, and dreamed about the gridiron, about catching the snap and turning the ball so the laces are just right to throw that perfect spiral, and now I question if this is what I still want. Being here with Cassidy has muddied the waters, turned my black and white world into a landscape of solid gray.

My mood continues to deteriorate as I drive home, and when I open the mailbox, there's a letter addressed to me. I don't pay too much attention to it, but then my phone rings, and it's my agent calling. He's the last person I want to talk to, but to avoid him wouldn't be good.

"Leo, what's up?"

"I called you earlier, but you didn't answer."

"Oh, I was in therapy. Must've missed it. What's so important?"

"Yeah, they want you back here."

"I thought we discussed that," I say, exasperation and annoyance coloring my tone.

"We did. But this is to evaluate your playing potential. They want to make sure you're roster-worthy."

"What? My rehab isn't close to being finished. I won't be ready until July like we discussed."

"Look, Fletcher, I told them that, but you know, they're covering their asses. If you can't play, they'll need to replace you."

"A lot of faith they have, huh?"

"It's all about the money. You know."

Yes, I do. And Leo is also about the money. This call isn't just about the coaches, manager, president, and everyone else who has a stake in the financial pie. It's about him, too.

"When?"

"End of May."

"Fuck." I'm not even sure that's possible. This will be my career-ender if I can't throw by then.

"Fletcher, you know you pissed them off when you didn't come back here."

"Fuck off, Leo. It's not like I had much of a choice. I have other responsibilities outside of the team."

"Whatever. You look at it one way. They look at it another. You could've hired a dog sitter and someone to watch your parents' house. Let me know when you're getting in. I'll pick you up at the airport."

"Yeah. Fine." I end the call and throw my phone across the room, scaring the shit out of the dogs.

"Goddamn cock sucking assholes. Take them to the playoffs how many times, not to mention to the Super Fucking Bowl and this is the thanks I get."

I toss the letter onto the counter and don't bother opening it. I know what it says. And then I take back all the thoughts I had before Leo called. No matter what, and even though Cass is the love of my life, I have to prove to them that I can do this. If they think they can take me out like some old wounded dog, they have another thing coming. But fuck, if this doesn't scare the shit out of me because I'm not sure if it's even possible.

The liquor cabinet and Jamison shout my name, so I head over and pour a glass. Before I know it, I'm four deep. Then I hear the gravel crunching as a car pulls up and the dogs start barking. Who the hell is that?

The door swings open, and a vision of loveliness rushes in.

"Are you okay? I tried calling, but it kept going to your voicemail," she says.

Shit. My phone. It's on the floor somewhere.

"Yeah, I'm fine."

"You don't look fine. What happened?" She crouches next to the recliner I'm sitting in.

My palm rubs over my hair, and I blink, trying to pull up the right words to tell her.

"You're scaring me, Fletcher."

I point to the counter. "There. In the kitchen. A letter. Just read the damn thing."

She walks over, and I hear paper tearing. After a couple of minutes, she asks, "Can they do this?"

"Oh yeah. They can pretty much do whatever the fuck they want. My agent called, so I don't have until July after all. Apparently, I pissed them off when I stayed. Fuck them." The whiskey was making me slur my words, and my thick tongue was getting the better of me.

"You don't mean that. But I'm worried if you try to throw too soon, you'll injure yourself. Can I write you a note?"

"A note to lose my contract, and then get let go from the team, you mean?"

"Okay, let's think about this. We have almost another four weeks. Your mobility is much better since we began. Your knee is still troublesome, but you'll have to keep wearing the brace, and all they want to see is your throw, right?"

My good shoulder lifts up. "You know what, I don't know what the hell they want. I think they want the team doctor to examine me while I'm there."

"Can I go?" she asks.

"You'd do that?"

"Well, yeah."

She stands there in her work clothes, looking as beautiful as ever, so I rise to my feet and wind my arms around her. "Have I told you how much I appreciate what you're doing for me and what you've done? I don't … I can't even begin to thank you. I would've been a miserable battered piece of shit if it hadn't been for you. God, you smell good—just like vanilla cupcakes. You wouldn't happen to have one in your pocket, would you?"

"How much of that stuff did you drink before I got here?"

"I dunno. A few glasses, I suppose."

Her body shakes as she says, "That's what I thought. Have you eaten this afternoon?"

"I can't remember."

"Come on." She tugs me into the kitchen and whips up some kind of tasty omelet. She serves it with toast and potatoes.

"Oh, God, this is the best food I've ever had. You should consider becoming a chef."

She laughs. "Is that a fact?"

I point my fork at her. "It is. You could open up a breakfast place and serve these omelets and that vanilla cupcake you're hiding from me. Where is that thing anyway? I want my dessert."

"Fletch, I don't have any cupcakes. It's my shampoo you smell."

"What? No cupcakes. I'm crushed. I was all set on having a cupcake. Hey, do you think we can bake some? Are they hard to make? I've never made cupcakes before."

She rummages through the freezer and comes up

with a container of ice cream. "How about this instead?"

"Okaaaaay. I guess it'll have to do. But will you make me cupcakes tomorrow?"

She shakes her head. "You and your cupcakes."

After dishing out a big bowl of ice cream, she sets it down in front of me. "What, no chocolate syrup?"

Her eyes move toward the ceiling, so I look up there to see what she's looking at. "What's up there? A bug?"

"No, Fletch. Forget it. Here's your chocolate," she says, pulling it out from thin air.

"Awesome. Wanna bite?" I hold up the spoon loaded with some of the cold creamy stuff. She opens her mouth, and I decide to be funny and play airplane. I swoop the spoon around, and somehow it misses and lands on her shirt, right over her boob. "Oops."

"You did not just play airplane and drop that on me."

"I thought that's what I did." I wear a sheepish look, or at least that's what it feels like. I touch my face just to make sure.

"All right, Fletch. Finish up. It's bedtime for you."

"You gonna read me a story?" I ask.

"Only if you're good and finish your ice cream real fast."

In record time, that bowl is empty, and she helps me get into bed. But the sad thing is, when my head hits the pillow, I can't keep my eyes open long enough to hear her story. The last thing I remember is feeling her soft lips touch my cheek. God, I love her lips. The best things ever.

CASSIDY

His eyes are closed as his mouth merely murmurs the words. But my heart soars like one of Fletcher's perfectly thrown passes when I think I hear him say he loves me and that I'm the best thing he's ever had. I'd seen several of his games as a professional player before I couldn't bear to watch anymore. He has the million dollar arm he's known for, which only reminds me of what I have to do to get him back on the field even if it means he will leave me brokenhearted again.

His soft snores give me the will to say the words I've been holding inside.

"I love you, Fletcher."

In his half-drunken state, he manages to snag me around the waist and murmurs back, "I love you, too."

If only love were enough. The hold he has on me is firm, but not at all uncomfortable. I allow myself to settle in, fully dressed as I am, and drift into sleep.

I dream of a house with mountains in the background with kids' voices coming from somewhere behind me far in the distance. Then it shifts, and his hands are on me. Damn, if he's the only guy to know how to touch me and where. Waking to find his mouth between my legs, I have no time to be self-conscious as an orgasm shatters through me before I can even say good morning. And then he's inside me, and that's when I realize I'm naked. When had the man undressed me? Truthfully, though, I'm not at all mad. He's slow, passionate, but relentless as he works me into oblivion.

Later, much later, I get him back with a bazillion punishing reps as he lifts low weights to retrain the muscles what they need to do.

"You're trying to kill me, aren't you?" Sweat pours off him, and it's so damn sexy and not at all gross.

The sweet smile I give him isn't so sugary as it is tart when I reply, "If that's what it takes to get you back on the field."

He groans while we work for another hour until we both reach our breaking points. His eyes are hungry, and I want to feed him. But I dash out of the door with a hasty goodbye instead. As much as I crave his touch, I need an escape. I'm starting to feel the early signs of dependency, and I can't allow myself to get that close. He'll be leaving before I know it, and the life I've built is here. And there's no way I would ever ask him to stay.

The rest of the week, I play dumb and coy, anything to keep things light yet business-like between us. I sense his growing frustration and try to keep my own at bay. Continuing to have sex with the man is like a drug I don't want to give up. So I'm avoiding it as a way to stop myself from falling any deeper with him than I already am.

It's late Friday evening when I have him flat on his back as I do therapy on him. I bend his thigh to his chest, flexing his knee as far as it can go without hurting him or his chances of recovery. When I let go, I stand straight.

"Well, your range of motion is much improved. I think that's enough for the day. I'll see you Sunday," I say breezily.

I make a break for the door, but the guy is fast and catches my wrist easily.

"What do you think you're doing? You can't put weight on your knee like that," I admonish him.

"Then stop running."

Sighing, I step over and help him back to the table from his place near the door. Then his hand is in my hair until he cups the back of my head. His mouth descends to mine, and my knees are the ones in trouble now because they can't support me. His kiss is sweet and kind and everything I need. I surrender for a second, grabbing hold of his biceps so I don't fall.

When I finally pull back, I lick my lips, not wanting to forget his taste.

"Fletch—"

"Cass, don't. You know how I feel about you. Stop fighting this."

I search his eyes and find nothing but love, and it hurts like hell.

"And we both know why you're here. And why I am, too. My job is to get you back to Oklahoma and on the field where you belong. And I'll still be here working as a therapist. When this is done, you're gone. And I can't let myself be broken again like the last time."

Tears prick the back of my eyes as I double time it to the door. Because more than anything, I wish things could be different.

"Wait," he calls out.

Not stopping, I glance over my shoulder. "I'm going to be late anyway. I'm going out tonight."

"What?" he growls. His voice is low and dangerous. "With who?"

"Does it matter?"

And then I'm out the door, running for my car because I know he can't run after me. I turn off my ringer and head to Gina's.

"What's going on?" she asks when she opens the door.

"I thought I would get ready over here. Besides, I don't have anything to wear you'd approve of. And I can't afford to buy anything. So maybe I can borrow something of yours."

Her eyes narrow because she knows me.

"What? Did you get in a fight with lover boy?"

My face screws up in an *are you kidding me frown*, and I wave her off. Moving past her into the cramped space, I try to sidestep all her shit.

"You're becoming a hoarder, you know that?" I ask, trying to deflect her question.

"Don't start with me. My place is too small."

"Exactly. Why do you need all this stuff anyway?"

She rolls her eyes. "Because I have friends like you who think I'm a department store. Come on. Let's see what I can convince you to wear."

An hour later, I look less like myself and more like Gina's long-lost twin. I push up the girls as I stare at myself in the mirror.

"Are you sure this won't fall down while I'm dancing?"

Her shoulders lift. "We can hope. Maybe flashing the right guy will get you in a better mood."

I stare at the ceiling and silently beg for patience. "I'm not looking for anyone. I've already told you that."

"Of course, you're not. You're just trying to forget about a certain quarterback with eyes like diamonds only for you."

I glare at her, starting to put two and two together.

"That's the best you've got? Where are all the four-letter words with creative add-ons you normally use for him?"

"Pfft. He's not that bad. Besides, maybe he has some friends."

An exasperated puff of air whooshes out of my mouth. "You are not on his side, are you? I thought you were my friend."

"I am. That's why I sanctioned this night. Does he even know you're going out?"

"He's not my keeper," I snap. She arches a skeptical brow, and I deflate like a wilting balloon. "Kind of. But I may have led him to believe that I was going out on a date."

Her head shakes. "You're going to kill him, girl."

"Am not. Besides, it's better this way. The weaning can start now."

"What, are you breastfeeding him now?" She laughs. "Of course, you are. Didn't know Fletcher was a breast man not an ass man."

Arching my neck, I try to look at my ass. "Is it bad?"

"You should ask him, not me. And while you're at it, maybe you should consider leaving town? Maybe you should give it a go with him."

She doesn't have to say go to Oklahoma for me to know her meaning.

I glare at my friend. "I'm beginning to believe you are in league with him. Did he pay you to like him?"

Because she's never been his biggest fan even when we started dating in high school.

It's her turn to wave me off. "Please. I'm looking out for you."

"You know I bought the practice, and I'm not just going to leave. Why do you think the doctor gave me a deal I could afford? That's because no one else wanted it. So, who will I sell it to?" I can see in her eyes she thinks I'm making excuses. "Whatever. Let's go already, because honestly, I can't breathe in this outfit. And my bed is so calling my name."

She holds up two fingers. "I forgot something." Quickly, she ducks inside her room. Seconds later, she mumbles something.

"Are you talking to yourself again?" I tease, saying it loud enough so she hears me.

"No, I just stepped on something."

That is totally probable since she doesn't know the meaning of a closet. Her floor is used for that. She says something else I can't decipher before exiting her room and saying, "Let's go."

A short drive later, we find ourselves at a club. The place is packed, and I feel old. I'm probably only a year or two older than most in the crowd. But once you've left college, clubs seem juvenile or maybe it's just me.

"Here you go," Gina says, bringing our rum and Cokes.

I toss it back, needing something to help loosen me up. I feel uptight. Or maybe it's the bustier and leather pants Gina crowbarred me in.

It isn't long before a guy with light brown hair and a winning smile heads in our direction.

"Hottie, two o'clock," I murmur, longing for another drink.

If he's here for me, I'm determined to talk to him, even though I don't want to.

"Ladies." He's all toothy smile and dimpled cheeks.

Gina turns around, and I watch as her eyes briefly

grow to the size of quarters before she narrows them. Does she know him?

"Ryder."

Hearing the name, I make the connection. He's Fletcher's cousin, and he sure has grown. I've only seen him once or twice because he lived on the West Coast. His eyes sweep over her. "Gina, looking good. No surprise there."

Her tone is flippant, but guys seem to like that, especially when Gina uses it. "I didn't think I'd see you again."

I ping-pong my gaze between them. "Yeah, I got traded. I'm here in the Carolinas now." His head tips in the direction of some stairs. "You should come up to the VIP area."

"Free drinks?" she asks.

"Anything for two gorgeous ladies."

She shrugs. "Okay."

He turns, and I mouth, "That's Fletcher's cousin. I didn't know you knew him."

Her eyes flick back to him, and so do mine. His backside is as impressive as his front.

"I'll tell you later," she whispers.

We head up to the VIP area, and sure enough, drinks are flowing. And there is more than one player in the room. Ryder introduces us to some of his teammates for the newest MLB team, the Carolina Cougars. They came to the mountains to celebrate a night off. What makes me happy is not seeing Fletcher. I'm weak when it comes to him.

Drinks flow, which help get my body moving. Hands on my hips and a beat that makes me want to move turn the night into something fun. Whispered words into my ear and I feel the guy against my ass is hot for me. The fact that I'm dancing and having a halfway decent time almost makes my heart believe I'll be okay when Fletcher leaves.

Only, I glance up and see him. *Fletcher*. He's here. I soak up the sight of him dressed all in black, looking like a sexy bodyguard. Then I see them. He's surrounded on all sides by women dressed in clothes that leave nothing to the imagination. Reality check, I glance down at myself, thinking what a hypocrite I am.

"Damn, girl, you are sexy as fuck," my dance partner whispers.

Well, if that isn't the splash of cold water I needed. I pull out of the player's grip.

"I'm sorry. I need to use the restroom," I mutter to him.

In reality, I'm fleeing, which it turns out is something I'm good at. Gina's wrapped up in Ryder, and I'll text her when I leave the room. I get to the stairs without Fletcher noticing me. At the bottom, a guy turns, and I think *what the fuck is my life*. But it's not like there are tons of hot clubs in the area. It isn't a surprise that he'd be here trolling for whatever. I wonder if his girlfriend is here, too. But that thought dies because I really don't care.

"Cassie," my ex slurs the word as some of his drink spills over the rim.

He quickly slurps it down as I stare in horror. He's a total contradiction, handsome yet I see the sloppiness that no one else notices. His eyes are glassy as they do their best to focus on me.

"You look good. But that was never your problem. Dance with me."

It's a testament to my own alcohol-numbed state when his hand is already at the small of my back. I'm about to pull away, when Fletcher comes into view walking down the stairs. So I reluctantly let Calvin guide me into the throng of people moving with the music.

I'm so focused on Fletcher and the gaggle of women following him that I don't notice Calvin has positioned himself in front of me. He tugs on my waist until we are flush with each other. He sucks in a breath that highlights how close we are.

"I miss this. I miss you."

Fletcher is downstairs, and because of his height, I can still see him. Surely, he'll see me when his gaze lands in our direction. I quickly look at my ex.

"Let me go, Calvin," I warn, before finding Fletcher again.

But it's too late. His lips are on mine, and I watch as Fletcher's gaze lands on us. It is as if Karma hates me. I see the events coming, but it's too late to stop them. Our eyes meet, and I watch in agony as he slings an arm around one of the women staring adoringly up at him.

His eyes shift to Calvin, and I glance over to witness Calvin's smug expression. I turn from Calvin. I turn from Fletcher. Then I barrel my way to the ladies' room, locking myself in a stall before my mascara leaves tire tracks down my face.

FLETCHER

The night, which was once again orchestrated by Gina, turns into a monster of a train wreck. Seeing Cass in those leather pants makes me mindless with lust. It's all I can do not to carry her out of there and rip the damn things off her so I can fuck her until she is as stupid as I am. But no. She has to run out of there with her hair on fire, and so what do I do? I follow her like a dog in heat, with my damn groupies in tow. I wish those fidiots would get lost for good. The annoying gnats won't take a hint, either subtle or obvious. Honestly, I could throw rotten eggs at them and they'd keep coming back for more.

But then the ultimate in a fucktastrophe of a night occurs when I get downstairs. Cass is standing there with that douchebag of an ex-husband of hers. How can she possibly want him? He's a loser in uppercase for fuck's sake. He needs rehab from what I gather, but then the drunken assface actually kisses her. And what does she do? Nothing! That's what. And then I really free the moron in me. The arm that dangles at my side instantly appears around one of the unnamed groupie's shoulders, and she starts giggling as she snuggles close to me. Cassie's eyes meet mine from across the room, and the wounded look she wears razors right through me. But what's worse is that fucker who holds her. His conceited little sneer makes me want to plow my fist straight through his face until it lands on the back of his skull. It goddamn rankles to no end that little squirrely piece of shit actually got her to carry his name. Son of a bitch. With nostrils flaring, I stride to the exit, because if I don't, blood will be spilled, and it sure as hell won't be mine.

"Slow down, hot stuff. These heels of mine won't let me walk that fast," little miss groupie whines.

Without a word, I disengage myself from her, and she squeaks, "Where you goin'?"

Anywhere but here, I want to yell, but I say nothing. The truck sits in the parking lot, and I don't stop until I climb inside. Logic tells me my knee should ache, but the only thing I feel is the crushing of my heart beneath my breastbone. And that is way worse than any injury I've ever sustained, on or off the field.

My phone starts to ring, but I ignore it. There is no one I can think of that I care to talk to right now. Reasonable conversation isn't in my capability. The only thing I want is to get home and drink myself into oblivion. I can't understand why Cassidy would do that.

Is being with me so distasteful that she would prefer her ex-husband? And if that's the case, then what does that make me? Talk about a lethal blow to your self-esteem. *Christ.*

When I pull into the long driveway, I'm already tasting the Jameson. Boomer and Brady act like I've been gone for a month. At least somebody loves me, and it sure as hell isn't Cass. I let the pups out and head directly to my favorite place to pour myself one hell of a glassful.

My phone rings again, and I ignore it. It's not that I don't want to talk. I *can't* talk to anyone. This head fuck I've been delivered is too much for me to handle right now. I need to sort this out first. And I'm not sure if I ever will. Right now, the way I feel, if she wants the ex, fine. He can have her because I can't and won't deal with the wishy-washy shit.

When the sun rises, I find myself in Dad's recliner with an empty glass in my hand. Boomer and Brady are barking outside. I must've really gotten plastered to let them stay out all night. My head feels like a grenade exploded in it. What the hell was I thinking? When I stand up to let the dogs in, my phone tumbles to the floor. That's when I notice all the missed calls. Sixteen to be exact. Most of them are from Gina. A couple of them are from Ryder. And one is from Cass. Why the hell would she even call? What in the world would she want with me?

Checking my messages, I realize I need to tell them I'm okay. I text Gina and Ryder, but Cassie is another story. I'm not sure I can bring myself to talk to her. Leaving a message entails expectations that she doesn't deserve. I can't deal with what's between us. I want something permanent, but if she doesn't, then I need to go forward, forget her, and put all this behind me. This heartbreaking thing every other day is absurd. How can I get over her if I keep prolonging the moment? I gave myself such a false sense of hope all for nothing. Had I known she still may be interested in her ex, I never would have carried on like that.

And when I think about the whole thing, it pisses me off. I should've gone back to Oklahoma like everyone wanted me to. But no. I stayed with the hopes of getting back with Cass, and look where it's gotten me. Now I stand an excellent chance of getting canned, and I've lost the girl, too. Halle-fucking-lujah.

My phone rings again, and I'm so damn annoyed I pick it up without looking at the caller ID.

"What?"

"Christ, Fletcher. Calm down."

It's Gina. "Sorry."

"I'm calling to check on you," she says.

"I'm fine. You've checked."

"What happened?"

"Maybe you need to ask Cass that," I say.

"I have, and she's behaving like you. She won't tell me a thing."

"I guess kissing her ex didn't do it for her then."

"What the fuck are you saying?" she asks, sounding

horrified.

"Exactly what you think I'm saying."

"She was kissing Calvin? She hates that slime ball. Why would she do that?"

"You'll have to ask her. I'm not a mind reader. And seems to me if she didn't want to kiss him, she wouldn't have."

"Fletcher, there's more to this. Trust me."

"Whatever. I'm done, Gina. I'm going back to Oklahoma as soon as my parents get home."

"Don't you dare." She sounds as though it's an order.

"Why the fuck not?"

"What about all your talk of love?"

A bitter laugh escapes me. "What love? All I've been hand delivered is pain, and I've had enough of that to last me a lifetime."

"When?" Gina asks.

"When what?"

"Are you leaving?"

My parents are due back in a few weeks, so I can't leave until then."

"Please don't do anything rash, but give me some time. And I swear there has to be an explanation for this. If you even knew how much she despises the fuckturd, you would know."

"She sure has an odd way of showing it."

"Besides that, what about your therapy?"

"I'm going to see if I can find another therapist."

Gina huffs into the phone, "You know she's the only

one in town pretty much. You'll have to go all the way to Asheville."

"Then fine. I can manage that."

"When's your next session?"

"It's supposed to be this afternoon. She was doing work for me on the side."

Gina asks, "What do you mean by *was*?"

"I'm not sure if I'm going."

"You have to go. Don't you want to get better?"

"Well, yeah. But I also don't want to torture myself either. Besides, I have the shits of a hangover."

"Hmm. Came home and tied one on, huh?"

"What do you think?"

"Fletcher, go to therapy. Call me later."

She hangs up, and I'm left trying to make a decision. The bottom line is I need to get better, and who am I kidding? This will be every bit as uncomfortable for her as it will be for me. I'm in.

When I show up, she's already there, and I relax a little. There was a part of me that wondered if she would stand me up. I walk inside, and the place is empty since it's the weekend. My knee bothers me some with all the damn striding I did last night as I head to the back.

"In here, Fletcher." I follow her voice to the conference room. She sits at the table and says, "Take a seat." Her hand indicates where I should sit, which is across from her. I ignore it and take the seat closest to her. I want her to squirm. But she's not playing my game. She jumps up and says, "I need to lock the front door."

When she returns, she takes the seat across from me. I let her have this moment, but I'll get her back some way.

"I ... we need to talk."

"I doubt there is anything we have to talk about. I would prefer to get down to business."

"But—"

"Cassidy, you made it perfectly clear where your interests lie last evening."

"No, I ... that's to say, it wasn't like that."

"So, you're telling me I didn't fucking see you kissing your ex. Is that correct?"

"Yes. No."

"Which is it, Cassidy?" Impatience is clear in my tone.

"Neither. He kissed me, and I pushed him away, but I guess you were too busy with your groupies to notice."

"Back to that, are we?"

"Yes! No, I mean, I saw you leave with one."

"Like I saw you kissing your ex?"

"Dammit, will you listen for once? *He* kissed *me*."

"And you let him. You two were awful cozy on the dance floor."

She huffs, "Again, his doing, not mine. I pushed him off me. But you left before you saw that."

"Just like you saw my groupie and me, huh?"

"This is all a misunderstanding."

"No, this is you screwing with my head, and I don't like head games."

She doesn't utter a word, but I can tell she's fuming

as much as I am.

"Let me tell you something. I am this close to ruining my career," I pinch my thumb and index finger close together, "because I opted to stay here with you as my therapist. And do you know why? I'll spell it out for you, if you haven't gotten it already. Because I wanted to convince, persuade, or whatever, you to believe that we could work as a couple. I love you—have never stopped loving you—since day one. And then last night I see you kissing that dickface. Yes, I may have put my arm around that woman, but I did nothing more than that. Quite honestly, I don't even know her name. I left the club in such a hurry I'm not even sure what happened to her. Can I help it if a damn pack of women hang around me? Should I pepper spray them? Tell me what to do that's legal in order to get rid of them, and I'll do it. But I don't go around kissing them for fuck's sake. To see you with him, well—" I throw my hands up in the air and shake my head in disgust because there is nothing left to say.

"I'm sorry. I swear to you I did not initiate it. He did."

"Did you push him away from you or try to stop him? I can't understand how he could've kissed you without your permission, especially when you didn't appear to be struggling to get away."

"I was in shock, I guess. But I did push him away, only you didn't hang around long enough to see it. Look, I can't keep repeating this. It was screwed up, I know. But I did not mean for it to happen. I can't stand Calvin and would never allow him to kiss me."

"It really ripped to see you with him, Cass."

"I know. I'm sorry."

There's not much more for either of us to say on the subject. I can't say I feel better about it, because I don't. At least not yet. On a positive note, she really does hate that douche ass of an ex of hers. The hurt is still there, though, and I rub my chest as though that will make it feel better. But I need to put this whole damn thing behind me if I'm going to move forward.

"I wish we could start the night all over," she says.

"Yeah, that makes two of us. Would you avoid me like I had a contagious disease again?"

"No. That was my first mistake of several. But what were you doing there anyway? Were you stalking me?"

I laugh at that. If she only knew Gina's involvement in this whole thing, she'd really be pissed at her best friend. "Actually, Ryder called me. You remember him? He's my cousin."

"I didn't until last night. I'd only met him a time or two."

"Yeah, well, that's because he lived on the West Coast. Anyway, he just moved here to play this season." I inch to the edge of my seat and ask, "What have I done to scare you off? You ran out of there without so much as a hello."

"You being Fletch scares me off. We just don't belong in each other's worlds."

"I don't think you give love enough credit," I say.

"Oh, Fletch, you don't make this easy."

"Who said it would be easy? But aren't things you have to work hard for worth it in the end?"

She has no answer to that. We finally make it to the therapy room where we talk a little more between her torturing motions.

"Think about it, Cass. Think about us. And what we could have together. And stop lying to yourself."

Later, my cousin, Ryder, calls.

"What the hell happened last night?" he asks.

"Long story that amounts to a misunderstanding, dude."

"You two are okay then?"

"Yeah, maybe. Getting there anyway. You remember Cassie, right? I dated her in high school and college."

"That's right. It's all coming back to me. It's been a while. Glad you got things straightened out because Gina was freaked."

"Yeah, it was the fucking circus. But things are better. So, how do you know Gina anyway? I didn't realize you two were a thing."

"I'm not sure we're exactly what you'd call a thing. But, yeah, back when I was getting signed, I came to visit your parents, and that's when I met her. She was working at The Dirty Hammer one night when I was there. She's pretty cool. And by the way, sorry I wasn't able to give you a hand after your accident. It was right when I was in the process of moving to Charlotte, and then we started spring training."

"Hey, I get that, man. No explanations needed."

"But another reason I'm calling is I want you to come to the game next weekend. I'll get you seats in the box, and afterward, you can come to the family room where the players join their families and friends. I'm going to call Gina and invite her as well. I wanted to give you a heads-up because I'm pretty sure she'll invite Cassidy."

"Yeah? I think the ladies would love that. I'm not sure if either of them has ever sat in box seats before. So that would be cool."

"It's a Saturday afternoon game, so hopefully, Gina can get it worked out. Maybe it'll help you score some points with your girl."

"Hey, I need all the points I can get."

"Cool. Hopefully, I'll be seeing you next weekend."

"Yeah, and thanks. I owe you one if it works out."

CASSIDY

A tense week goes by between Fletcher and me. I get the feeling he's pulling back, as he hasn't pressed me about a commitment anymore. There should have been relief from that, but there isn't. When I head to pick up Gina to go to the baseball game, I have a feeling Fletcher will be there.

"What's with the frowny face?" Gina asks, buckling her seatbelt.

"Nothing."

"Sure," she says. "Haven't had sex all week, have you?"

I glare at her because she's right, and I am grumpy. "Why is it always about sex with you?"

"Sex is good when the right guy is doing it."

"And is Ryder doing it good?" I say, turning the tide of the conversation.

She shrugs. "He's worth a repeat performance."

Gina is tight-lipped when it comes to herself, so she

hasn't yet told me the deal between them. "And when was the first time?" I ask.

"He was a mistake. A pretty boy. You know I don't normally go that way. I like them rough around the edges. But I don't know. He caught me on a good night. And I'll be honest and say it was worth one night of bliss."

"And now?"

Sighing, she says, "Now he got us seats in the team box at his home game, but that doesn't mean I'm giving him anything more. He's cute, but so not my type."

"Is that why you're dressed like a normal person today and not some sex siren?"

She glances down at her jeans and T-shirt and shrugs again. I, on the other hand, had spent an hour trying to decide. We're going to be sitting in the box, which from my understanding is a pretty big deal. It kind of feels like I should be more dressed up. Then again, it's a midafternoon game. That's why I decided on a flirty spring dress because it wasn't exactly hot out.

From our arrival all the way to our seats is fancy. Ryder hooked us up with valet parking, and we'd been ushered to a lower level where a fancy restaurant lies hidden below with access only to those with the right tickets. Interesting to see how the other half lives. We're given the choice to eat at the elegant buffet, for free mind you, or take the elevator to the box level where food and drinks are also served.

"Let's go up," Gina suggests, picking up a glass of

wine before we do.

I follow suit, nerves getting the best of me. What if Fletcher is around, but he's not alone? I have a feeling he's given up on us. My worst fears are realized when we walk into the box. The view is amazing, but Fletcher stands in the corner talking to a striking woman I've never seen before. Gina steers me to the other side of the room like a good bestie should.

"Don't let him get to you, girl. If he's moved on, fuck him. That means he wasn't ever worth your time."

I nod, fighting the urge to bolt. So, I sit in the front row of leather seats facing the field and focus ahead. The game is already underway, and I try to figure out which team is on the field. Gina leaves me to raid the buffet table on the back wall. I slowly sip my wine I snagged from downstairs. It tastes as bitter as I feel.

Even though I'm staring out the glass, my nerve endings fire up as he approaches. I glance up to see he's brought the stunning dark blonde with him.

"Cass—"

"Fletcher." It's rude how I say it, but it's hard to see him with someone else even if I know we can never be together.

He smiles at me and gives a brighter one to the woman at his side.

"Riley, this is Cassidy. Cassidy, this is Riley, Ryder's sister and my cousin."

My foot desperately wants to come off the floor and insert itself into my mouth. Though I manage a politer,

"Hi, nice to meet you."

Riley isn't stupid. She senses the tension between Fletcher and me. "It's nice to meet you, too. Will you excuse me? I see that my dad just walked in. Let me go greet him."

She walks away, and, man, don't I feel like a royal ass. Fletcher eases in the seat next to me, taking care with his knee brace. That gives me ample time to come up with an apology.

"Sorry. That was rude of me. Guess I'm a little bitchy today."

"Just call it what it is, Cass."

"And what's that, Fletch?" I snap.

"You were jealous."

I fish-mouth for a second, wanting to deny it, but in the end, I don't. "Fine, I was jealous."

He takes my hand. "You have nothing to be jealous about. It's you. It's always been you. And always will be. You make me crazy at times, but how many times or ways do I have to say it to get you to believe me?"

It's no use trying to tug my hand away. He won't let it go. "I believe you. I just wish you played for Carolina instead."

"So, if I get my agent to work on that, will you give us a shot?"

I shake my head no, and puzzlement crinkles his brows. "It's not that. We have to get you healthy. And honestly, I don't want to you resent me or regret something later by changing your whole life for me."

He nods, and it's my turn to be disappointed he's given in so easily. "Then let's enjoy ourselves while I'm here. Who knows, a long-distance relationship isn't a bad thing. We could try again."

"Fletcher—"

"Cass, let's not debate this. It's not like I go around sleeping with women. I can hold out for you. But let's not discuss the future now. Let's just be together today and let tomorrow come."

It would hurt like hell to have him walk away from me at the end of this journey. Then again, it would hurt to have him walk away now; might as well enjoy him for a few more weeks.

When I nod, he draws me into a kiss that gets us a round of applause. My cheeks burn, especially since Fletcher takes that opportunity to introduce Gina and me to Riley's family, whom Ryder had flown in for the game. Later, Ryder knocks one out of the park, and I watch Gina's eyes go dreamy. She and I need to have a serious talk. She's more into Ryder than she's letting on.

That night I pant with Fletcher between my legs. Damn, the guy knows how to eat pussy like I'm a smorgasbord.

"I'm close," I call out.

He only becomes merciless when he shoves another finger inside me, curling it enough to touch that spot inside that makes me unravel. My insides splinter, and I lose focus. His jeans are already off when he sits. He pulls me onto his lap with my back to his chest and raises me up to shove inside me. Too much time without him shows. He feels larger than life as he stretches me to the breaking point.

"Ride me, baby."

He leans back, and I do just that, hard. I'm determined to break his dick if I have to in order to get off again. I've become a greedy girl when it comes to Fletcher Wilde. He doesn't seem to mind either. In fact, his hand cups my ass as he repeatedly slams me down as his dick rams the end of me. It should hurt, but the slight pain only makes me wetter.

"I'm going to have to buy you a new couch," he says smugly, still thrusting into me.

But I don't have time to think about it. He pinches my nipples, and I ignite. As I become boneless, he takes over, using his bruising grip on my hips to keep up the friction. When he groans, exploding, I lean back, tilting my head for a kiss.

His arms wrap around me, and we reposition ourselves. He doesn't pull out, and I'm okay with that as I drift off to sleep.

Fletcher briefly wakes me later because he has to go feed the dogs. I opt not to go with him. When I'm awakened later by loud raps at the door, I think maybe he's come back. I walk to the front entrance and peer through the peephole. Calvin stands, or rather shifts on his feet, on the other side.

"What do you want, Calvin?" I ask through the door.

"Let me in, Cassie."

"It's late, Calvin," I say, using his same annoyed tone.

"It's my house, too, and I got kicked out. I need somewhere to sleep."

"Sorry, I have company," I lie.

"Who's there? That football asshole?"

Who in town had been running their mouth?

"It's none of your business. Go to a motel."

"I don't have money."

Of course, he doesn't.

"Sleep in your car." It's mean, but something seems off. And I can't let him in.

"My car's in the shop."

All his answers are too quick and clipped.

"Why?"

"Busted radiator, what do I know? I'm not a mechanic. At least let me borrow some money."

"Borrow some money? I don't have any extra money. You got credit cards in my name and maxed them out, leaving me to pay them off. So, no, I don't have any cash on me." Also another lie or at least the part about not having *any* cash.

His fist hits the door, rattling me, too. I jump back.

"Let me the fuck in, Cassie, or give me some goddamn money."

I don't want to admit fear, but I feel something close to it. Calvin may be a drunk, but he'd never hurt me before, not physically at least. Who is this man?

"I'm calling the cops."

An idle threat, I hope. Last thing I want to do is

announce to my neighbors I have trouble.

"Will she do that?" It was a different voice and male. "I thought you said you could get the cash you owe me from her."

"Shh," Calvin whispers and not to me.

He'd brought someone else over here in the middle of the night? "I'm calling them now!" I shout.

I move away from the door, intending to do just that.

"Fine, I'm leaving. But this isn't over!" he yells.

How many of my neighbors had he woken up? But a quick check out the window and I watch him get into a dark sedan with some other guy. When they pull away, I finally relax. Well, sort of. What the fuck was that all about? My hands shake as I make my way to my bedroom. I almost call Fletcher, but I decide against it. Calvin's gone, for now. No need to wake Fletcher up. Plus, I have to be able to take care of myself.

Sleep eludes me for the rest of the night, yet somehow I'm still late to work. Fletcher, my first appointment for the day, is already in the room when I walk in.

"Sorry," I say.

"You look tired."

"Thanks," I say, but there's no teasing tone in my voice like there is in his.

"I kept you up too late."

"It's not that," I snap. I realize I've made a mistake and gently add, "Let's just get started, okay. I have a full day."

I'm writing notes on my clipboard when he snatches it away. Good thing I hadn't started carrying around the computer to write notes the way he tosses it onto the counter nearby.

"Don't," he growls and pins me to the wall. "Don't do this again. I thought we agreed."

I can't answer before his kiss steals my breath. His hands tighten on my hips when Jenny starts knocking on the door.

"Sorry to interrupt, but you're needed up front right now." I hear through the closed door.

Shoving at Fletcher because Jenny sounds panicked, and she never sounds that way, I'm out the door in a flash. When I round the corner, Calvin is heading in my direction.

"Where are you going?" I'm so pissed I want to throw something, but I also can't afford to replace anything either. In the last couple of weeks, I took the plunge. I managed to get a loan to buy the business from the doctor who was selling. I hadn't told anyone. And my cashier's check has barely cleared, and now this.

"I've come to see our business. Just got back from the bank and guess what I find out?"

Fletcher is behind me. Although I hadn't heard him, I feel his heat at my back. "What?" I snarl.

"That you've taken a second mortgage out on our house."

"*My* house."

"I went to try to get a loan on the house."

"You what? You can't." Words launch out of my mouth haphazardly. "The house isn't even in your name anymore."

He shrugs. "But you owe me my half of it. And I hear you're using the money from a second mortgage to finance this place, which means half of this place is mine."

How the hell did he know that? Who at the bank had told him my business?

"Get out!" I yell, not caring if anyone else sees this debacle.

"I don't—"

"You heard the lady," Fletcher says, cutting him off and moving to stand almost in front of me. "Get the fuck out."

"Oh, lookie here. The asshole that destroyed my marriage. Do you know how many times I came home to her crying over something on TV? It took me a while to figure out why SportsCenter and TMZ would make my wife cry."

Those times had been few and not by choice. But turning on the TV and catching Fletcher on the news those couple of times had reminded me of all I had lost and made me more determined to avoid mentions of him for that very reason.

"And now you're back with your fancy shit." His wild eyes land on me. "He's just going to fuck you over again, Cassie. Meanwhile, why don't you get him to give you the money to pay me off? And I'll gladly stop bothering you."

Calvin spins and leaves while I'm left there wondering what the fuck just happened. Jenny's wide eyes are on me. Fletcher turns me to face him.

"I'll give you the money."

I shake my head. "I don't want your money. I never did."

"I know, and I love you for that. But let me do this."

Snorting at the unreality of this moment, I say, "If I give him anything, then he'll do this the next time he's in a jam, and he'll just come over like he did last night."

"What? He came to your house last night?" he bellows.

Not a single bit of work is getting accomplished, so I tell him what happened.

"You're staying at my place until we sort this out."

"I can't," I say, not really having a good reason.

"Either you stay with me or I'll stay with you."

FLETCHER

Seeing the way that dickface speaks to Cassie makes me want to not only smash his pie hole to smithereens, but also flatten that motherfucker until he can't get up again. The idea that he went to her house last night, while she was there alone, almost makes me lose my shit. But when I hear the douchebag talk about how I destroyed her marriage, I nearly kiss the guy. It comes as a huge shock to me because I hadn't been aware she'd even seen so much as a clip of a game, much less watched me on TMZ. It doesn't negate his foul treatment of her, though. She's not safe, and I aim to rectify that.

"You decide, Cass, but I won't have you staying by yourself while I'm here. I see him as a huge threat to you. I … Jesus, that fucker could've hurt you."

"He won't. He doesn't have it in him. He's not a bad guy. He's just in a bad place."

"I think you're in denial. Look at the way he charged

in here. Did you see your admin's face? She was frightened out of her wits. Desperate people do things they normally don't do."

Cassidy is proud, and I get that. She's probably balking because she doesn't want to admit she's afraid, and I get that, too. She may see it as a weakness, but she is not that at all.

"How do you think I would feel if something would've happened to you and I could've prevented it? Let me help you. Please, Cass. Besides, Boomer and Brady told me to tell you they miss you."

She looks up at me with a playful half-grin and says, "You're not going to let up, are you?" I shake my head. "Fine. But I'm only doing it for the dogs. I feel sorry for them having you as their only caretaker."

Letting her have her fun, I pull her in my arms and hold her for a long minute before whispering into her ear, "Thank you." Putting a tiny distance between us, I give her a pointed stare. "Now, are you going to tell me why you never called to say you still had feelings for me?"

Shyly, she graces me with those beautiful golden eyes of hers. Only now pain and darkness mar the brightness that was there moments ago.

"Can we talk about this tonight? I probably have a patient or two waiting, and in all honesty, this won't be an easy thing for me."

"Sure. What time will you be ready?"

Her expression clouds with confusion. "What do you

mean? I know where you live. I can drive."

"I understand that, but I don't want you driving out there alone. I'll meet you and follow you."

She smirks. "Fletcher, I'm a big girl. I'm pretty sure I can handle the drive."

"I'm a big boy, but I'm pretty sure I want to escort you."

After a large harrumph, she finally gives in, and I leave so she can resume her work. She says she'll make up my missed appointment tonight. It's all I can think of all day long. So to get my mind off her, I give my buddy, Mark, a call to catch up with him.

"You back in town?" I ask. He's been away on a business trip to the West Coast.

"Finally. What's been happening?"

"Not too much." I fill him in on my situation with the team.

"So, what are your plans with Cassie after you prove yourself?"

I let a laugh out, but it's not exactly a humorous one. "You may have to ask her that." I explain what's been going on with Cassie and me, physical therapy and otherwise.

"I always wondered why she married that loser. Have you met him?"

"Sure have. He came in her workplace just today. Dude, I guess you missed a lot while you were gone." So, again, I have to give him the lowdown.

"Hey, Fletch, don't you remember what a soap opera

this town can be?"

"I guess I was too young when I lived here to have thought about it like that."

"That and your damn head was in the shape of a football or in Cassie's puss—"

"Careful, man, you're treading on thin ice."

"Sorry. I was only joking," he quickly says.

"I'm the only one who can joke about that stuff."

"I've got you, man. So, wanna grab some lunch? I'm free for a change."

"Sure, and you can fill me in on Cassie's ex. I need the scoop on the dude since he's threatening her."

"I'll give you all I know, but it's not much."

We meet at the same deli Gina and I did, and Mark tells me what he knows. Apparently, the guy's an alcoholic and cheated on her. Everyone in town was shocked when she married him and not me. They all claimed it was a rebound thing. Now my guilt is sky-high. After he lost his job, he didn't treat her well—not that he abused her or anything, it just wasn't great.

"I'm going to talk with her about all this tonight," I tell Mark.

"Do you think she'll be up front about it?"

I raise and lower my good shoulder. I'm still babying my injured one. "We'll see. I want her, Mark. I want us to work. I always wanted us to work. She's the one who pulled away, broke it off."

"That's not the way she sees it."

"She freaked when she saw all the women, but it

was all a media stunt."

"Yeah, you lucky dick, you," he says, laughing.

"That would be right up your alley, and if you weren't such a traitor, I'd get you to one of our games."

Still laughing, he says, "I can be turned."

"Renegade bastard." We both laugh this time.

"I gotta get back to my desk. I'm so behind on paperwork, it sucks."

"I don't envy you."

"Hey, one day when you can't throw anymore, you'll be stuck behind some giant desk, too. Then you'll see how the poor people live."

"You are so full of shit. Poor, my ass." Mark is one of the biggest brokers in the area and does extremely well.

"Compared to you."

"I don't spend. I save, so when the day comes, I won't be broke like so many pro athletes end up."

"Don't I know." He says that because he's my broker.

We part ways with promises to catch up later. When it's time, I head over to Cassie's office to follow her home. We stop at her house so she can pack an overnight bag, but I encourage her to bring enough clothes for several days. And then we head out to my place. Boomer and Brady almost knock her down because they're so excited to see her.

"Didn't I tell you they missed you?"

"Do you ever pay these guys any attention?" she asks.

"Of course. They just love a pretty woman, like I do."

I start to pull a bunch of stuff out of the refrigerator.

"What are you doing?" she asks.

"Preparing dinner."

"You?"

"I've lived alone for quite some time. While I don't enjoy cooking, I know how to do it."

"Hmm. This will be interesting."

I walk outside to turn on the grill. While it's heating up, I chop up the vegetables for the salad and check on the potato casserole that's been in the oven since I went to pick her up. It looks about ready, so I turn the oven off and let it sit in there to stay hot.

When the salad's finished, I take the beef filets out to the grill to cook. On the way, I ask, "You still like your steak medium rare?"

"Yes, thanks."

When the steaks are cooking, I set the table and pour the red wine that's been uncorked and breathing.

"Wow, Fletch. This is impressive."

"Can you light the candles, please?"

"Sure. Where are the matches?"

"Over by the fireplace."

She takes care of that while I pull the steaks off the grill. I plate everything and place it on the table, along with the salt, pepper, and salad dressing.

"Dinner is served."

I seat her and then myself. When she cuts into her steak, I watch to make sure it's cooked properly. Overdone beef is not acceptable. She eyes it and then declares it's perfect so I am satisfied. The deal is sealed when I taste mine.

"This is really delicious, Fletcher. Thank you."

"Glad you approve."

"You've been holding out on me."

"No, not really. You haven't been around much or you would've discovered this sooner."

After we both finish eating, I ask, "Cassie, why didn't you ever tell me?"

We know each other so well that I don't have to explain my question. She places her napkin onto the table and says, "It was ... difficult on me." Her eyes are focused on her lap, and I'm not sure if she's afraid to show me what's in them or if it's because what she's about to share with me is too painful to say to my face. "I would see you on TV and—" She holds up her palm toward me because I get ready to interrupt her. "Hear me out, Fletcher."

"Okay."

"You say it was a media thing. But it wasn't to me because I didn't know that. I *couldn't* know that. What I saw was you surrounded by all those beautiful women, hugging you and draped all over you, and you standing there acting as though it was the coolest thing ever. It crushed every piece of me. After the first time, I told myself it was for publicity, like you said, but then it kept happening, and the whispers around town every time I walked into a room, it was—" She shakes her head as though it were the most distasteful thing in the world.

"Can you put yourself in my shoes even for a minute?"

Jesus. After I clear the knot out of my throat, I say, my voice gruff with emotion, "Yeah, I can and it feels damn shitty."

"So for a while, I watched you from a distance. But then I stopped. I had to. It was like mourning the death of a loved one, if you want the truth. Calvin didn't lie. He'd come home a couple of times and caught me crying like a baby over some replay from one of your games on ESPN or some stupid news release of you on TMZ. I was an absolute mess until I decided to focus on work. I poured everything I had into it. Which leads me to where I am right now. And why you and I are on parallel roads to nowhere, because they will never intersect, Fletcher. Not anymore. It's too late for us."

"You can't know that. And why do you say we're on parallel roads? I refuse to believe that!"

"Because we are. My life is here, especially since I just bought the practice, and yours is in Oklahoma with your team."

"Cass, we can make this work. I know we can."

"How? You're on the road a lot, aren't you?"

"Yeah."

"So, when will you ever have time to get back here? A couple of months every winter? And I can't up and leave at the drop of a hat. I have a practice and patients to see, too."

I want to sling my wine glass across the room, but I don't because it will only create a pile of broken glass I'd have to clean up and wouldn't solve a single thing. When I look at it from her perspective, she's dead ass right.

"Then what do you suggest we do, because I don't want to give up on us. I love you, Cass. I've never stopped loving you, and I know in this heart of mine, I never will."

"Never is a long time, Fletch."

"Look at us. After all this time, I feel every bit the same about you as I did the day I first laid eyes on you. I knew it then, and I know it now. I was young and naïve back then. But I'm not anymore." I pick up her hand and bring it to my lips. Right before I do what she thinks I'm going to do, I turn it palm facing up, and press my lips there. "You'll never find anyone who is more loyal, loving, caring, trustworthy, and who will protect your heart for the rest of your life like I will. I promise you that."

"I know, Fletcher. That's what makes this so damn difficult."

"Then say the word. Please come back with me."

"I can't. You know I can't."

"Yes, you can."

But I know by the sadness she holds in her eyes that she won't. She'll come with me for my demonstration, but that'll be it. I'm going to have to find some other way to persuade her. What that is, I have no idea.

CASSIDY

With his brace off, Fletcher stands before me bending his injured knee in a lunge position. I watch like a proud mama. He bends a little further to pick up the football at his feet. Next thing, he's sending the ball in a beautiful spiral my way. I catch it, wanting to jump up and down in excitement, knowing that I've done all I can for him. He will either prove his worth to his team or I'll look like the worst physical therapist ever.

His eyes dance as he stalks toward me. "Am I good, doc?"

Tears threaten to fall. "You'll do well tomorrow."

"All thanks to you. I'm not gonna lie. These past few weeks have been brutal, but I'm as ready as I'll ever be. We should pack."

Pursing my lips, I give a slight smile. "You should. I'm not going, Fletch."

His face falls. "Cass—"

I hold up a hand. "Let me explain. While I'd love to go with you to watch you crush it..." He smiles. "I have appointments. I don't have someone to take my clients in-house. If I send them somewhere else, I risk losing them to my competition."

"You could have told me." His tone carries an accusatory ring, and he's right. I could have.

"I tried to see if Cory could work his schedule in my favor, and he couldn't. You were so happy about me going, I didn't want to say anything until I'd exhausted all my options. I'm sorry. Really I am."

And it's not the whole truth. He doesn't know how much I've agonized over how to make this work between us, the distance. How we could both have our careers and be together. And I came up empty unless I give it all up.

I squeal when he scoops me up into his arms. "If you're not going with me, then I have to get my fill before I go."

He jogs up the porch stairs into the house and doesn't break stride, with the exception of opening and closing the door. The dogs think it's a game and make chase. But once we reach his room upstairs, they aren't quick enough before he closes the door on their excited faces. I almost feel bad until he dumps me onto the bed.

His shirt is off in one swift motion. Then he hooks a thumb in the waistband of his shorts, making my mouth water.

"See something you want?"

I mumble a yes.

"Show me that pretty pussy of yours, Cass."

Damn, if he couldn't make me wet by just talking. I squirm out of my workout pants under his lingering stare.

"No panties, Cass?" His brow arches.

I shrug. "I didn't see a point."

"Fuck, if I'd known that, I wouldn't have finished that workout."

"But now you can finish me off."

"I want to taste that sweet pussy. Face down, ass up, Cass."

Like a wanted woman, I get in that position, feeling vulnerable, but safe at the same time. The bed shifts, and then his hot mouth tastes me, making my eyes roll back. His tongue slides through my folds but goes a bit higher, and I shudder.

"Fuck me, Fletch," I beg.

"And what do I get if I get you off?"

"Whatever you want," I say mindlessly.

"What if I want to share you, Cass?"

Before I can answer, he shoves into me, and his thrust makes any questions disappear off my tongue. But he isn't done.

"Have you ever been fucked by two guys?"

His hand is on my shoulder, pressing me to the mattress. I'm barely able to shake my head as the idea makes my pussy quiver. Then I feel the invasion as he presses a finger inside me.

"Imagine it," he says as his strokes become ruthless and punishing.

And I do. The faceless guy in my head stands before me in my imagination as Fletcher fucks me from behind. That's all it takes to push me over the edge screaming because his thumb finds my clit at the exact moment.

A couple more punishing thrusts and he empties himself inside me. He collapses on top of me, flattening me to the bed. I don't mind. His warmth envelops me as the heat on our skin slowly cools.

"Don't get any ideas, Cass. I'll never share, even if the idea intrigues you."

I say nothing because it does, though Fletcher has no problem getting me off.

When I wave goodbye to him the next day, I try to convince myself the only reason I agreed to stay at his parents' place is for the dogs. But the truth is, I feel safe in his sheets on the bed the two of us shared.

"What do you say, guys? Up for a walk?" I say to Boomer and Brady as their tongues hang from their mouths. I toss the stick, and they take off.

Fletcher is only supposed to be gone for a few days, and I'm already lonely without him. I'm in the kitchen filling the dogs' bowls when the call comes.

"Mrs. Miller?"

An hour later, I'm still shaking as I drive into Bransonville. When I pull into the inconspicuous shop, I have no idea what I'm in for. The office is staffed with a kind looking older woman.

"May I help you?"

"Yes, I got a call from my insurance adjustor about my car?"

"Are you okay, dear?"

I nod. "I'm Mrs. Miller."

My name seems so ordinary as I say it, but it feels so foreign on my tongue.

"Ah, yes. Would you like to see it?"

I give her my silent agreement. The car isn't mine, and I'd almost gotten exasperated with my agent trying to explain that the car didn't belong to me, but my ex-husband. After he explained why the car was in the shop, I had to see for myself.

"Here it is."

And there it sits. The breath rushes out of me as I stare at the thing. The hood of the car holds a large dent, and the windshield is splintered with a million cracks, yet holding together. The kicker is the huge dent in the front near the radiator that easily resembles the straight shape of a leg at impact before a body would be tossed in the air to land hard on the windshield.

"This is your car?" the woman questions.

We trade a few more questions and answers before I leave.

Rage clouds my rational mind as I drive home. That isn't exactly my destination. I make a call before I pull up at Calvin's last known address. I have no desire to talk to his girlfriend and have managed not to do so until now.

The door opens a crack, and a woman with hair that

looks bleach fried answers the door. Her face withers into hate when she recognizes me.

"What do you want?"

Never could I understand what Calvin saw in her. He can talk circles around her. What do they talk about at night? Then again, my ego isn't seeing the bigger picture. She's better in bed than I was. At least that's his excuse to me.

"He ain't here, if that's who you are looking for."

There isn't a reason to debate. "Where is he?"

"Don't know. Don't care."

The door closes in my face. I have no choice but to leave, so I drive back to Fletcher's place and let the dogs out. I fill their bowls before getting into my car and going back home. I check the streets for cars I don't recognize before I get out. My keys rattle in my hands because I'm still reeling over the news. I close and lock the doors, leaving my purse on the table by the door before heading into the kitchen.

"There you are."

Calvin's arm is a steel band around me, pinning my arms at my sides. And the metal at my neck tells me I've been wrong about him. He is very capable of hurting me, and this time he means me harm.

"I've been waiting for you to show up. Have you been with him?"

He actually gives me a sniff, which makes my stomach revolt.

"What are you doing?" I ask, sounding calmer than I

feel.

"Cassie, I never wanted to hurt you, but I have to choose my life over yours."

Spikes of fear stab at my chest. "What does that mean?"

He edges me toward a chair that looks as though it's been waiting for me. I'm shoved in it, landing hard and awkwardly. I turn to straighten myself out so I can see what's happening.

"Don't test me, Cassie. I don't want to hurt you."

He holds some wire hangers he's undone. I sit quietly as the cold blade is pressed to my neck. "Twist this around your wrist and the chair." There's determination in his eyes. Rising anger has me snatching the proffered wire from his hand, and I twist it around like he expects me to. Once I'm done, he does my other wrist and comes back to secure the one I did so I can't move and feel it pinch at my circulation.

"Calvin, what are you doing?" I ask again.

He leaves and comes back with my purse. Dumping it onto the floor, he finds my phone.

"What's your passcode? I need to unlock it."

When he'd been on the floor, I'd considered kicking him with my unbound feet. However, he'd been just far enough away, and I hadn't been sure I could have done it. I decide to hold that card until I have a for sure shot.

I do what he asks, even knowing what's coming next. Calvin may be book smart, but he's criminal dumb. This is playing out like some movie he's watched. He has to know there is no way he can get away with this. But I say nothing.

He scrolls through my contacts until he finds the one he wants and makes the call.

"Sorry, this isn't your baby, " Calvin says.

Fletcher's enraged voice comes through, but barely distinct. He's obviously yelling. Today is the day he's supposed to meet the coaches. I'm surprised he's answered his phone.

"Yeah, well, if you want her back in working order, you'll stop demanding and start listening."

There is a pause.

"Good, now I want you to bring me a million dollars cash." Calvin listens for longer than I imagined he would. "Makes sense. Twenty thousand then." He nods to no one. "Fine. Don't tell anyone or bring the cops. Otherwise, she dies with me. And I'm not going to jail." Another pause. "I think you know where. You have twelve hours." Pause. "You're a guy of means. Find a way."

He hangs up and smiles at me. "You've really got that guy all wrapped up, just like you had me."

I harrumph. "If I had you, why'd you cheat on me?"

The answer isn't really important. But maybe if I can appeal to the guy I used to know, I can get out of this.

"I thought you understood my end game. You knew my plan for the future."

"Wind turbines," I say matter-of-factly.

"Exactly. Clean energy. I get that land, and I get the

investors. We would have been set for life. I didn't plan on the old man having a daughter he wanted married off. So I seduced Tara. I had no choice. I'd borrowed money that needed paying back. She turned out to be a good lay. I told you all of this."

He had, but it seemed ludicrous. The truth is, he banged her because he wanted to and hadn't denied it.

"I asked you to sell a number of times. You didn't. I held off the guys as long as I could siphon money from the old man for..." he makes air quotes, "my wedding with Tara, the farmer's princess."

"You borrowed money from a loan shark."

Shrugging, he says, "No one believed in me. You didn't believe in me."

"I did. I just didn't see how you would finance this."

"I needed a little capital. Besides, it's too late for all that."

"And you brought a loan shark to my house," I say, thinking of the night he'd shown up.

"No!" He looks at me incredulously. "That was the guy that sells me the coke. I need that to take the edge off, you know." No, I didn't. "We did have good times, and maybe we can have more."

"You aren't the man you once were. I don't know why you've fallen so far." Anger makes me say things I shouldn't. "You so easily gave up on a million dollars for twenty thousand. Or maybe that's all I'm worth."

It's dumb to think that way, but who imagines themselves in this situation. I laugh, trying to fight back tears.

"Oh, you're worth it to that asshole. He's willing to wire me the rest of the money. He just can't ask the bank for a million dollars in cash on short notice."

Duh, which shows how coked up Calvin must be.

He steps closer to me. "Maybe if I got you pregnant, you'd forget about that asshole and stay with me."

There is no fucking way I'm going to let him touch me, so when he gets close, I kick out. He tumbles back, and I get to my feet hunched over. I barrel forward.

"No fucking way!" I shout. "And I know about the car. You're the one who hit Fletcher."

Impact. He crashes back down from where he tried to stand. And the damn chair is made too well that it doesn't fall apart like they do in movies. The fall throws me off balance, and he lands a kick to my gut. The air leaves me, and I gasp.

"How'd you find out about the car?"

I'm sucking in a breath, and it takes me a moment to wheeze out, "Insurance agent."

"Of course," he says, getting to his feet. "I couldn't pay the deductible to get it fixed."

Now I'm sure of his idiocy. If he was trying to hide the fact that he'd had a hit-and-run, why had he contacted our insurance company?

"Sorry about this." Something hard hits my temple. Instead of seeing stars, I sink into darkness.

I wake to the sound of ringing, but it's not my ears. The doorbell. I have no idea how long I've been out. Only the aches from lying on my side on the hard floor tell me it's been a while.

Sideways, I watch as feet find the door. Fletcher barges in, sending my door to crash into the wall on the inside. There is a scuffle, but he groans as his knees buckle. His hand reaches for his recently rehabilitated knee, and I have to guess that Calvin landed a blow there.

Calvin brandishes a gun and levels it at Fletcher's head. "Where's the money?"

"Out on the porch."

Calvin fires and I scream as Fletcher falls face first to the floor, but he isn't out of the game quite yet. His leg lifts, and Calvin goes sprawling out the door. Then I hear it.

"Freeze!"

FLETCHER

Leaving Cassie and getting on a plane to prove my worth and that Cassie's rehab worked is harder than I thought. Leo waits for me at the curb in his shiny black Escalade when I exit the airport. He's all white teeth and grins, but when I climb into the car and shut him down, he doesn't get it.

"Fletch, you should be happy to be back and out of the sticks. Come on, man."

"Cut the bullshit, Leo. You know damn well I'm pissed about this. You fucked me over, man. The coach did, too."

"Fletch, baby, they have to know you're roster-worthy."

Gritting my teeth, I say, "If I hear you say, 'Fletch, baby,' one more time, you're fired."

"But, Fletch B—"

"I'm not even joking, Leo. This is not a fucking picnic. Do you know the rehab I've been through? I'd like to see you even come close to doing what I've done. Now shut the fuck up and drive."

His yammer opens and closes a few times, but he decides his best option is to say nothing and puts the SUV in gear. It's a good thing, too. The last thing I want to hear is his grating voice. When he pulls up in front of my house, he puts his car in park.

"Don't bother getting out. We have nothing to say to each other." I grab my bag out of the back and head inside. I'm done with his ass, and I'm looking for a new agent.

In the morning, I'm on the field bright and early. I want to get this over with. The day I'm scheduled to throw and give my demonstration isn't until tomorrow, but fuck that. They want me here. I'm here. Let's do this.

Coach comes up to me, along with the quarterback trainer, the offensive coordinator, the general manager, and the president of the team.

"Fletcher. Looking good," Coach says.

"Feeling great," I say with exaggerated exuberance. "I'm ready for my demo."

"You're scheduled for tomorrow."

"Yeah, but I'm here. You all are here. Let's get the show on the road, why don't we?"

They all share glances. Then Coach asks, "What about Leo?"

"What about him?"

"He's not here."

"Fuck him." I don't add *he won't be hanging around*

me much longer anyway.

The offensive coordinator says, "I'm cool. You guys? Coach?"

"Yeah. Warm your arm up, Wilde."

I nod and do some exercises and then toss the ball a few times, maybe fifteen minutes worth, until one of them comes and gets me.

"Ready?" Coach asks.

"As I'll ever be."

We go out onto the field, and they ask me to demo several different kinds of passes, of which bullets and Hail Marys seem to be the two they want to focus on. Probably because those are the ones that require the most strength and accuracy. My precision is dead-on. After I don't know how many, because I lose count, they tell me it's enough.

I walk to the sidelines, and the offensive coordinator comments that he's never seen me throw so well. "I don't know what you did, Wilde, but keep it up. You looked great out there."

The president and Coach are low talking, so I don't do anything except walk to my bag and fumble about, waiting for one of them to tell me something. Finally, Coach tells me to come back the next day because they want to talk about next year.

"Am I good for now?" I ask.

"Yeah. Nice work."

"What time you want me here?"

"Nine."

"See ya then."

That night, I go make some contacts about getting a new agent. I need someone who has my back and not just his. After a few calls, I strike gold. Or at least it feels that way. We have a long discussion about our respective needs, and I send him over my current contract with Leo. It's nothing that I can't get out of without a thirty-day notice. I made sure of that when I signed with him.

I take care of some things at the house that need attending, along with talking to Cassie, but the next morning I'm up early and at the field again. I don't let Cassie know a thing about what happened. I want to surprise her with the news when I get it.

The coach is interested in seeing how well my knee is doing. "I know you can throw, but what about pivoting and all that?"

"I'm okay. I have a bit more healing to do, but I'll be prime when training camp starts."

"Can you lunge yet?"

"Yeah," I say, "but I have to be careful. As you can see," I point to my knee, "I'm still in a brace." Then I show him how much I can do.

"Good. Come on." I follow him into the office where the general manager and president wait.

"Morning, Fletch," they all say. I nod in return.

The president starts out by saying, "We were all impressed by your progress. To be honest, we thought you'd be warming the bench all season, and we were even prepared to trade you."

"Yeah, I figured as much." So much for having faith in their players.

"But after yesterday, we are prepared to offer you another contract, even though this isn't your year," the general manager says, while the others look on and I'm waiting for their tongues to hang out of their mouths.

"Look, I really appreciate it. But before I can do any signing, I need to check with my girl back home."

Coach's face turns a dusky shade of purple as he speaks, "Girl? What'dya mean *girl*? Why would you check with anyone on something this huge?"

"Because I made a few mistakes when I first signed, and I won't make those same mistakes twice. The fact is, there's more to life than this game. Don't get me wrong. I love this team, and I love football. But I love my girl more. So like I said, let me get back to you on that."

Coach holds up his palm. "But you aren't considering another team, are you?"

"I can't say."

The general manager stands up and says, "We'll raise you, Fletcher. And before you sign with anyone else, come to us. We'll make it financially worthwhile for you."

I scratch my head a second. "Can I ask you guys something? When I was injured, and you didn't know if I was coming back, did you even for a second give a shit about me and everything I had done for this team in the past?"

The crickets are chirping as loud as I've ever heard them.

"Yeah, that's what I thought." I turn to leave, and as I open the door, I say, "I'll let you guys know." Maybe this isn't the team for me after all. I'll have my new agent on the lookout for something. When this upcoming season is over, maybe I'll be picked up by another team. And maybe it'll be close enough to home so that Cass and I can figure a way to work things out.

My bag is on the field, so I head on over and pick it up. On the way home, I really start to think about things—how important football is in comparison to Cass. I piddle around the house, putting things in order, and no matter what I do, the fact remains that I won't be happy unless Cassie is with me. Tomorrow I return to my parents' house. They will be getting back from their trip to Europe this weekend. And then I'll be free to do whatever I want. But the thing is, I want to stay there until training camp. Being back here makes me realize exactly how lonely I am. My friends are few, and I don't have a life that exists outside of football.

With my head wrapped around this subject, it barely registers when my phone rings. I answer it right before it goes to voicemail, and I'm glad I do because it's the one person in the world who makes me happy.

"Hey, baby."

"Sorry, this isn't your baby."

The voice turns my blood to ice in my veins.

"What the fuck is going on? If you touch one hair on

her head, I swear to God I'll knock your teeth all the way into your brain, you slimy piece of shit. Let. Her. Go!" I'm roaring into the phone. I'm surprised my neighbors haven't heard me. Then that shithead demands I bring him a million dollars.

My molars crack as I grind them to death. "That's impossible!" I yell. "Though I'd bring you ten if I could. The bank will only let me withdraw twenty grand at a time. Unless I get preapproval and that takes a while." My hand scrapes my hair back. Jesus, if that fucker hurts Cassie, I'll be in prison for his murder.

Then he tells me I have twelve hours to do this.

"Twelve hours? I'm in Okla-fucking-homa! How the hell am I supposed to do that?"

Oh, he says I'm smart and that I'll figure it out. And I will even if I have to charter a jet. I get on the phone, and that's exactly what I end up doing. Chartering a jet. I go to the bank and make a withdrawal and then come back here, where I order an Uber. I have no idea how long I'll be gone this time, so I don't want to leave my car out there.

On the way back to Cassie, I ignore the motherfucker's warnings about not calling the police and call them anyway to let them know what's going on. We're on the phone the entire flight back, but I make it well within the twelve-hour window. The trip has done nothing except fuel my anger. Cassie will never suffer at that douchebag Calvin's hands again. I don't care if I have to kill him tonight. That dude is going down.

When the plane lands, I'm surprised to be greeted by two FBI agents who escort me to their waiting black SUV. *Just like in the movies*, I think, as I sit in the backseat. We drive to their headquarters, and I tell them everything again. They explain that they believe Calvin is holding Cassie in her own home. The plan is for me to go to the door, with my money as a distraction. I'm to coax him out onto the porch, where the agents will arrest him.

"How will I get him out there?"

"Set the money out there. He'll automatically go look for it," one of the agents suggests.

"Do you think he'll be armed?" I ask.

"We don't know that."

"I don't want to barge in there and risk Cassie getting shot."

"Mr. Wilde, if you don't act, he's going to suspect something, and her chances of getting out of there unharmed decrease with each passing moment."

"Okay." I'm not overly confident in this plan because I'm worried about Calvin's stability. He's not playing by the same rules as normal people do. But if I don't try, then she stands a chance of getting killed. My window of time is running out.

"Let's go."

One of the agents speaks up, "We need to wire you first."

Once I'm set, they run a quick test, and then we load up. They drop me off down the street and then circle the block, parking on the opposite end. It's getting dark by now, but I've got to hurry. My time is about up.

Following the plan, I ring the doorbell, but decide waiting for stupid fuck to answer is a mistake. So I do what any over-the-top, protective, mildly insane boyfriend would do. I kick the door in and rip it off its hinges. It crashes into the wall as I push it to the side, and shrimpy doodle is there to seemingly take me on. If this situation weren't so dire, I'd laugh at Mini Mouse. Except he levels a kick right at my bad knee and brings me down instantly. Fuck! Next thing I know, the prick has a gun pointed at my face.

"Where's the money?" Little Fuck asks.

"On the porch." The Feds were right about that one, thank God. But then, the little shit fires the gun, and burning pain momentarily renders me motionless. Except I'm not finished with him. Instinct overrides everything, and I kick my leg out right as he walks by, only he doesn't notice. He's too focused drooling over the bag of money. He trips over me and goes sprawling. I almost chuckle, but my head is on fire, and I have Cassie to tend to. He face plants in the middle of the doorway, just in time for the agent to yell out, "Freeze!" How perfect is this?

Crawling to Cassie, I undo the wire that's wrapped around her wrists and ankles and check her out. She puts her arms around me and starts crying. "Are you okay, Fletch? Did you get shot?"

"No, baby, I'm good. I'm worried about you."

"But you are bleeding." Cool fingers press the side of

my head. By now, the pain has subsided.

"It's nothing. I think the bullet only grazed me. But what about you? How are you?"

She's not convinced I'm okay. Her hands are all over me, on my head, face, and knee. "I'm fine. Just bruised and stiff from being tied up on the floor. Your knee. Is it okay?"

"It's fine. Just bruised, too."

The agents cuff Calvin and read him his rights. Then they come and check on us.

We get up, but they call an ambulance.

"We're fine."

"It's policy, Mr. Wilde. We need to make sure."

"Fletcher, Calvin was the one who hit you. It was him." Cassie squeezes my arm.

"What? How do you know?" She explains about her insurance agent and also that Calvin admitted it to her.

Part of me wants to strangle the guy for being the asshole who hit me. Then again, had he not, I wouldn't have gotten Cassie back. So maybe in some miniscule way, I'm grateful. Though when the FBI calls in the police to coordinate Calvin's charges for that unsolved crime, I'm thankful the fucktard will be off the streets longer.

"We believe Mr. Miller will be facing some serious prison time," one of the agents says. "We're glad they caught who did this to you, Mr. Wilde."

"Thanks." I pull Cassie close to me. To think she was alone with that man. "He could've killed you."

She looks up at me and nods. I run my hands through

161

her hair, not wanting to let her go.

The sound of the sirens is getting closer, so Cassie calls Gina to ask if she can give us a ride home from the hospital.

"What! What the hell is going on?" Gina screams into the phone.

Cassie sighs. "Just come to the hospital, and we'll fill you in."

"You two." I can hear her say.

Our diagnoses are the same, with the exception of the minor laceration on my head caused by the grazing of the bullet. We both have bruises. But the good news is my knee is fine. No damage at all.

"God, Fletcher," she breathes. "If he wasn't such a miserable shot, you would be dead."

I kiss her so we both know we're okay. "But I'm not."

We are released into Gina's capable hands.

"So, it was that shit, Calvin, huh?"

"Yeah," Cassie answers. "He was in my house when I came home. He was crazed I guess from all the coke he'd been doing."

Gina is strangely silent as she drives us out to my parents' house. When we get there, she comes inside and stands there with her arms crossed.

"What?" I ask.

"So, this is what happens when you leave? What is she going to do in July, when you go for good? Can we expect this to happen again?"

"Gina," Cassie says in warning.

Gina's hand flies out. "No, you know I'm right."

I take a step forward. "Yes, you are. But it's not going to happen anymore, because I've made a decision. I'm not going back."

Cassie's brows shoot up to her hairline. "You're not going back where?"

"To training camp. To Oklahoma. To the team. I'm done. I came to the realization on the flight back here when I didn't know if I would find you dead or alive that you are far more important to me than any football deal. So I'm staying here. With you. So we can be together." I beam.

If I thought she would smile in return, I'm terribly disappointed. Because she doesn't. Instead, the corners of her mouth pull down as she seriously frowns. But then, she's in my arms. When she pulls back, she wipes at tears.

In a voice that there is no arguing with, she declares, "Like hell you are. I love that I'm so important to you. Important enough that you'd give up playing, but I won't let you do it, Fletcher. You can't play football forever. In fact, you have what, eight, maybe ten to twelve solid years of playing left in your arm?"

"Cass," I warn. "None of it matters if I don't have you by my side."

"True. But your career is limited."

"I don't care."

"I do. And mine, on the other hand, is not. I may have started something here, but I realized something, too, when Calvin threatened my life."

"What's that?"

"I can be a physical therapist anywhere in the world. But there is only one you. And you mean the world to me. I won't make the same mistake twice. So, on that note, I'll go wherever you are." Now she's the one beaming.

"You would do that?"

"I would. We were both young and selfish back then. Look at how much time we lost being apart. I would have never married that asshole if I'd followed my heart to you."

"This is crazy. First, neither of us would bend. Now, both of us are willing to do whatever it takes."

Cass says, "Maybe we've finally grown up and realize what's important in life."

My arms are around her before I can even think. Her kisses are like the greatest things in the world. Okay, maybe not as great as her pussy, but whatever.

"Hey, break it up over there. You all have company," Gina teases.

Cass pulls away and says, "You're not company. You're Gina."

"Ah, yeah. I'm outta here."

We don't even wait for the door to close behind her before I pull Cassie's pants off and lift her onto the counter. I want that sweet pussy on my tongue and don't want to wait any longer. The idea that she may have been hurt sends me into a sexual frenzy, and my tongue laps her up until she moans her pleasure. I know she's damned pleased, too, because she just about pulls all my hair out. I unbutton my jeans and pull them off, and in one clean thrust I'm hilt deep inside my girl as she sinks her nails into my arms. Then I lift her up and walk her over to the wall where I plunge into her softness and lose myself. She wraps her legs around me as I grab her ass—God, I love this ass, but I'm so close so I want her to come again.

"Cassie, touch yourself for me. Now, while I've got you up here."

Her hand moves between us, and I feel it move on my dick as she presses it against her clit.

"Tell me you're close, baby. You're so good for me here."

"Ah, yeah."

A few more strokes, and she's there. I follow as I orgasm into her, feeling her tighten against me.

Her mouth is a mere inch away from mine, so I steal a kiss from her. Only we end up making out like we did in high school. "You always did have the sexiest mouth I've ever seen."

"I love you, Fletcher Wilde."

"I love you, Cassie baby," I say because I refuse to call her Miller anymore. "Can I ask you something?"

"Yeah. Are you interested in changing your name?"

"Ugh, yeah. I need to get rid of Miller and go back to my maiden name."

I laugh. "That's not what I was referring to."

A crease appears between her brows. "What do you mean?"

"I was wondering if you wanted to change it to Wilde?"

"What are you saying?"

"I think you know what I'm saying."

Her eyes linger on mine for long moments before she grins.

"Cassidy Wilde. I love the sound of that."

"So do I."

All of a sudden, the dogs start barking. And then we hear the sound of a car.

"Oh shit," Cass says. She wiggles out of my arms and runs to put her clothes on while I do the same.

"I wonder who's here."

Right as we finish dressing, Mom and Dad walk in.

"Fletcher. Cassie." They look at the two of us in surprise.

"Mom. Dad. How was the trip?"

"Great. Your brother is doing amazing over there. He loves Europe, but there are several American soccer teams who want him, so who knows?" Dad says.

My brother is a professional soccer player in Europe who's been trying to get back to the American league. Everyone, including me, says he's crazy, because soccer in Europe is like football over here. The money is better. Well, actually, everything is better. But I think he just misses being home.

"So, did we miss anything while we were gone?"

Mom asks. Then she steps closer to me and asks, "Fletcher, what the hell happened to your head? Have you been in a fight?" Her eyes swiftly move to Cassie and see the bruises on her arms, and she says, "Okay, someone better tell me what's been going on here. And Fletcher, why are you wearing that knee brace?"

Both Cassie and I burst out laughing.

"This isn't even funny." Then her eyes ping back and forth between us. "Are you two back together?"

About two hours later, we have them filled in. My mom is all tears. "Oh, Fletcher, I can't believe I wasn't here to help you."

"Mom, it's fine. I had Cassie. And look what happened. We got back together. Oh, and the best part of it all was she agreed to marry me."

"I did?" Cassie asks.

My face falls. "I thought—"

"You thought right, except you left something out," she says.

"What's that?"

"You didn't properly ask me."

I slap myself on the forehead, then immediately drop to my good knee. "Cassidy, I love you more than football, and you should know this because I offered to give it up for you. So, will you do me the greatest honor in the world and agree to be my partner and wife?"

"Yes!"

My dad smiles, and Mom claps.

"Oh, thank God, we're going to have a wedding at

last!" Mom hollers.

Cass and I kiss, and Boomer and Brady run around barking. I'd say it's a very good day after all.

EPILOGUE

The box is similar to the one we sat in for Ryder's game, yet it's different in some respects, too. There are more tables, and the furniture, although nice, is showing some wear. Then again, Ryder's stadium is new, and this one isn't.

"I could totally get on board living life like this," Gina says.

"Don't. This isn't where the wives normally sit. The owner is trying to sweet talk Fletcher into signing a contract extension. As such, we've been given this box for the home season opener as an incentive. I guess he thinks if he treats me nice, I'll have an influence on what Fletcher decides. He doesn't know us very well." I can't help but laugh. When my guy makes up his mind about something, nothing will change it. Besides, I'm totally on board with whatever Fletcher thinks is best for his career.

Gina shrugs. "Still. It's crazy sweet. And Fletcher's

house is amazeballs. Damn, I'm jealous, girl."

"It's only four thousand square feet. It's no mansion, which I'm happy about. I'm not sure I'm the mansion type."

"It's has five bedrooms, a game room, and a pool for Christ's sake. And let's not talk about all the acres of land that surround the place or the horses. Horses, Cassie."

I have to admit, I have started taking riding lessons. A childhood fantasy realized. But mostly, I secretly hoped Fletcher would be traded to Carolina, so I could be closer to home.

"And too big for two people, let alone one. We don't need all that space. It's just more for me to clean."

She waves me off. "Then fill it up with babies, or get yourself a housekeeper."

"No housekeeper. As it is, we are paying a widower to come in and fix Dad's meals and keep his house straightened up. She's a friend of Fletcher's parents who lost her husband a few years back. She never worked and needed something to do. And Dad needs looking after when I'm not home. You know how I worry about him when I'm so far away."

"But isn't he overseeing the renovation of the farmhouse you guys bought?"

"He is. I'm just glad my house sold. I was never going back there, especially after everything that happened. Fletcher insisted I use the proceeds to pay off Calvin's debts. That way I have no one coming after me. He wanted to pay it off, but I refused to use his money. But

SIDELINED

the money from the sale, well, it was part Calvin's money anyway, according to the divorce decree. And his parents don't deserve to be forced to pay the debts either. They're good people."

"Does Calvin know?"

"No. At least I don't think so. He's safe behind bars for a long time. And I've ignored the letters he's sent. I changed my phone number again, so he doesn't call me collect either." I stop when Gina turns toward the window before I decide to broach *the subject* again. "So, have you talked to Ryder?"

Her reply comes too quick. "Of course not."

"You know, you haven't gone out much recently."

She glares at me. "How would you know? You're only in town Tuesday through Thursday, and that's to work at your practice. Then you are gone on the weekends to be with your man. I barely see you anymore."

I had been taking a lot of flights. But after my name got in the paper for being responsible for getting Fletcher ready to be back on the field, my practice exploded. I had to hire another therapist to help with the overload of patients.

"But when I call or offer for you to come out here with me, you're on board. So there must not be anyone else. And you never really explained what happened between you two, especially that night at the club."

"He's like all the rest, Cass. Most of us don't have a Fletcher. His brother's in town, right?"

That's a match made in hell.

"You and Chase are like oil and water. Don't go there. Besides, I think he's trying to play soccer here for some girl he's head over heels for. But I've seen how you look at Ryder and how he looks at you."

She ignores my comment and sighs. "What is it with the Wilde boys? Hopeless romantics."

"What about the Wilde boys?"

I look up to see Ryder's sister, Riley. She and her brother are dead ringers for each other—light brown hair and blue eyes. No wonder they have to chase both men and women off with sticks with looks like they have.

"Hey, Riley."

She waves and takes a seat next to me.

Gina goes on to explain, "Fletcher and his brother, Chase, are like dogs with a bone when it comes to the women they love."

Riley jumps in. "Ryder's like that, too. Although he's acting all weird lately. I think he's into someone, but he's not talking. I've tried to pry it out of him, but he's super close-mouthed on this one."

I don't want Gina pissed at me, so I don't look at her after what Riley says. Instead, I ask, "Well, you're a Wilde girl. Are you a romantic?"

"Please. I believe in free enterprise. I mean, why is it okay for a guy to be called a manwhore and everyone back slaps him, but if a girl's called a whore, she's treated like a leper?"

Gina high-fives her. "I'm with you on that one."

They stare at me. "Don't look at me. I've had two long-term relationships. When have I had time to sow oats?"

They shake their heads. "At least you have one of the good ones. If he weren't my cousin, I would have jumped him."

Gina and Riley slap hands again, before Gina chimes in, "And what's with your wedding? I thought you wanted something small."

"I did. It's not my first wedding. Although, going to the courthouse doesn't count as a wedding, does it?"

Gina perks up. "Nothing you did with that fucker Calvin counts for anything."

"He wasn't always a bad guy. Don't make it seem like I had poor judgment dating him."

"Okay, he wasn't a total douche back then. But the guy was always a dreamer and had nothing to back it up. You could have done better."

"Can we not go there? It's done and over with, and I finally have my dream guy," I say.

Riley looks over my shoulder. "Oh joy. There's my brother. And he's brought *her*."

This time I can't help but look over at Gina. There is no mistaking that frown. Gina shoots up and announces, "I'm getting a drink. You guys want one?"

I shake my head no.

"Rum and Coke," Riley says.

"We are so going to get along."

Gina knocks fists with her before striding away.

"So, you're moving to North Carolina?"

"I am," Riley says. "A lot of tournaments happen on the East Coast. Plus, my brother hates living alone. And as his big sister, I'm obligated to take care of him."

"Big sister?"

"Yes, I'm older by two minutes. And, trust me, I feel two years older than him." We laugh until she says, "What is Fletcher doing up here?"

I turn to see my guy all uniformed up, standing in the doorway and searching the room.

"I'll be right back."

"Go get him," she says conspiratorially.

I rush over to him. "Shouldn't you be on the field?"

His eyes crinkle at the corners as he stares at me. Never in my life have I ever felt this loved. I could kick myself for almost missing this chance.

"I had to see you first. You're my good luck charm."

He draws me in for a kiss, not caring about the audience we have.

"You're going to miss the first play," I warn when he pulls back.

"We won the coin toss, so we're kicking off. Besides, there is nothing more important in the world to me." Then he splays his hand across my abdomen, sporting a smirk. "Unless, of course, I knocked you up last night."

"Stop." I laugh. "People are watching. Besides, I just stopped taking birth control. The doctor says it could be a while before my body aligns itself to be ready for a baby. And I can't get pregnant before the wedding."

He shrugs. "My boys are potent, Cass. And they've been patiently waiting for you. Besides, if we are going to have ten kids—"

"Ten kids?" I practically shout in alarm.

"My bad, eleven. We need enough for a team."

I playfully slap his hands away. "I'm not having a football team."

Fletcher puts a hand to his helmet, and I can tell he's listening to something.

"What's going on?"

He holds up a finger. Then he looks up with a grin on his face. "They've got me mic'd up this game." When I stare at him, he explains, "The helmet is fitted with a speaker and mic. And Coach just radioed I have twenty-five seconds to get my ass down on the field if I don't want to be cut."

"And what's funny about that? Go get to the field." I practically shove him toward the door.

"It's funny because twenty-five seconds has ruled my life. If the game is stopped because of an injury, we are given twenty-five seconds on the play clock to get off a play. And all it took was twenty-five seconds to change my life. And even though it was one of the most painful experiences I've ever had, I wouldn't have a do-over. Because it wasn't just the injury that sidelined me. You have been the something that was missing in my life. That accident, though I hated it at the time, brought us back together."

"Sidelined, huh?"

"Yes, *you* wrecked me. I love you, Cass, with everything I am."

He pulls his helmet of and kisses me hard.

"I love you, too, with my everything." I kiss him this time. Then I pat him on the butt like the players do. "Now, get your ass on the field before I sideline you again because that twenty-five seconds is up."

His mouth is hot on mine and he tugs me closer to his erection I love so much. "You can sideline me any day," he says before heading back to the field.

THE END

A THANK YOU

We'd like to thank you for taking the time out of your busy life to read our novel. Above all we hope you loved it. If you did, we would love it back if you could spare just a few more minutes to leave a review on your favorite e-tailer. If you do, could you be so kind and not leave any spoilers about the story? Thanks so much!

ACKNOWLEDGEMENTS

To every athlete out there, who dedicates hours and hours to their sport, we thank you and appreciate you. Not only do you entertain us, but you also give us something to write (fantasize) about!

To our readers: you guys are THE BEST! And we say that from the bottoms of our hearts. We love and appreciate each and every one of you and we hope our little dirty, flirty romance is something that you love. We decided to play a little with this and veer away from the serious so we could have some fun. So please tell us what you think. Hit us up on Facebook or wherever, but there will be more Wilde Players on the way.

Here are the lovely people we'd like to say THANK YOU to. Our beta readers: Kristie, Andrea, Nina, Kat, Jill, and Heather. You ladies are our shining stars and always make our books brighter and prettier than they can ever have been without you. We Love you to the end zone and then some!

Thank you Nina Grinstead, and Social Butterfly PR for running your butt off in getting our stuff out there when we were so late. We love you!

And thank you Rick Miles at Redcoat PR For everything, but especially for putting up with Annie (and Walter) after two pots of coffee. Next time she'll just give the coffee to Walter.

ABOUT THE AUTHORS

A.M. HARGROVE

One day, on her way home from work as a sales manager, USA Today bestselling author, A. M. Hargrove, realized her life was on fast forward and if she didn't do something soon, it would be too late to write that work of fiction she had been dreaming of her whole life. So she made a quick decision to quit her job and reinvented herself as a Naughty and Nice Romance Author.

Annie fancies herself all of the following: Reader, Writer, Dark Chocolate Lover, Ice Cream Worshipper, Coffee Drinker (swears the coffee, chocolate, and ice cream should be added as part of the USDA food groups), Lover of Grey Goose (and an extra dirty martini), #WalterThePuppy Lover, and if you're ever around her for more than five minutes, you'll find out she's a non-stop talker. Other than loving writing about romance, she loves hanging out with her family and binge watching TV with her husband. You can find out more about her books at http://www.amhargrove.com.

TERRI E. LAINE

Terri E. Laine, USA Today bestselling author, left a lucrative career as a CPA to pursue her love for writing. Outside of her roles as a wife and mother of three, she's always been a dreamer and an avid reader at a young age.

Many years later, she got a crazy idea to write a novel and set out to try to publish it. With over a dozen titles published under various pen names, the rest is history. Her journey has been a blessing, and a dream realized. She looks forward to many more memories to come.

You can find more about her books at www.terrielaine.com.

STALK TERRI E. LAINE

If you would like more information about me, sign up for my newsletter at http://eepurl.com/bDJ9kb. I love to hear from my readers.

www.terrielaine.com

Facebook Page: /TerriELaineAuthor

Facebook: /TerriELaineBooks

Instagram @terrielaineauthor

Twitter @TerriLaineBooks

Goodreads:/ Terri_E_Laine

Other Books by Terri E. Laine

Cruel & Beautiful

A Mess of a Man

A Beautiful Sin

Chasing Butterflies

STALK A.M. HARGROVE

If you would like to hear more about what's going on in my world, please subscribe to my mailing list at http://amhargrove.com/mailing-list/.

Please stalk me. I'll love you forever if you do. Seriously.

Website: www.amhargrove.com

Twitter: @ amhargrove1

Facebook Page:/ AMHargroveAuthor

Facebook:/ anne.m.hargrove

Goodreads:/ amhargrove1

Instagram: @ amhargroveauthor

Pinterest:/ amhargrove1

annie@amhargrove.com

OTHER BOOKS BY A. M. HARGROVE

Cruel and Beautiful
A Mess of A Man
A Beautiful Sin

The Guardians of Vesturon Series:
Survival, Book 1
Resurrection, Book 2
Determinant, Book 3
reEmergent, Book 4
Dark Waltz, A Praestani Novel
Death Waltz, A Praestani Novel

The Edge Series:
Edge of Disaster
Shattered Edge
Kissing Fire

The Tragic Series:
Tragically Flawed, Tragic 1
Tragic Desires, Tragic 2

The Hart Brothers Series:
Freeing Her, Book 1
Freeing Him, Book 2
Kestrel, Book 3
The Fall and Rise of Kade Hart

Other Standalone Novels:
Sabin, A Seven Novel
Exquisite Betrayal
Dirty Nights, The Novel